Project Nirvana

How the War on Drugs Was Won

Pyotr Patrushev

Second Edition

ISBN: 978-0692247150

Published by

Leaf Garden Press
LeafGardenPress.com

in association with

Peganum Books
www.pyotr-patrushev.com

Table of Contents

Foreword

I first thought about writing *Project Nirvana* in the sixties when I arrived in Australia as a refugee from Russia.

There was a personal reason to my choice of drugs and alcohol as a theme for *Project Nirvana*. My father and my brother were both alcoholics. Many of my Russian friends drank excessively. Although in Russia I never smoked or drank alcohol at all, I began to drink and smoke while in solitary confinement in a Turkish jail, where I was detained and interrogated after my escape from Russia. I was aware of the tremendous influence that alcohol had exercised on the Russian mind, body and spirit. I broke my drinking habit by starting to meditate. I struggled with smoking for many years and finally gave up tobacco when it became clear that it would destroy my heart and kill me if I continued to smoke.

All these strands of thought and experience came together when in the late eighties and early nineties I began working as an interpreter and consultant at the *Esalen Institute*, located on the West Coast of California. The *Esalen Institute* was and still is one of the leading institutions of psychological training and holistic medicine in the United States. Over the years, tens of thousands of people from all over the world attended Esalen seminars and went through long-term live-in volunteer programs. During the late eighties and early nineties, Esalen had a very active Soviet-American exchange program. Under its aegis well-known Soviet and American scientists and writers were allowed to interact in a free and uninhibited manner. These seminars were not only intellectual, but also experiential. The scientists took part in shamanistic and rebirthing sessions and indulged themselves in the world-famous Esalen massages and spas. One of the scientists whose work was important for *Project Nirvana* was Dr Stanislav Grof, a Czech-born psychiatrist who in the sixties conducted pioneering experiments with alcoholics using LSD-25. When the use of LSD became restricted, Stan shifted his work to what he called "holonomic integration," which involved rapid breathing and evocative music to provoke LSD-like experiences in his subjects.

Another participant in the seminars was Dr Andrew Weil who has now become probably the best-known longevity and holistic medicine practitioner in the United States. At the time he was involved in the exploration of psychedelic plants and their effects on human consciousness. A Harvard graduate, he taught medicine at the Arizona Medical School, and he even had a species of mushroom (*Psilocybe weilii*) named after him. In 1972 he travelled to a Mexican village where, under the guidance of a local *curandera* (a native Mexican woman-shaman), he participated in a healing ceremony. In this ceremony he consumed twenty-two specimens of *Psilocybe cubensis* ("magic mushrooms") and later reported that the *curandera* considered the mushrooms to be the *gran remedio cure* (the great healing substance). My discussions with Dr Weil and during a trip to an American-Indian sacred place in the Arizona desert (see photo on the back cover) had a profound influence on my thinking.

I was an avid yoga and meditation practitioner in those years and was against the use of any drugs, plant or otherwise. However, as I lived and worked as a radio correspondent in California, drugs were all around me. Dr Alexander (Sasha) Shulgin was my neighbour in Berkeley. One day he dropped a vial of pills into our kitchen table, saying that this is something we might enjoy taking. Shulgin is now credited with popularising *MDMA* (street name "ecstasy"), especially for the treatment of depression and *post-traumatic stress disorder*. Sasha was a leading psychopharmacologist who worked both for the government and for large pharmaceutical companies. He told me that MDMA and similar drugs could open people's hearts, and may even bring "peace on Earth". I took his claims with a grain of salt as I distrusted all chemicals and did not really believe that anything at all could suddenly bring "peace on Earth" after thousands of years of violent human history.

But the strongest influence that finally made me sit down and write *Project Nirvana* were my meetings and conversations with Dr Aron Belkin, director of the *Moscow Center of Psychiatric Endocrinology* who also conducted research into drug addictions.

He told me about a project they had discussed at the Institute. The project was to rescue the native inhabitants of the Kamchatka peninsula, on the Far Eastern seaboard, from being wiped out by vodka. Kamchadals, as the natives of Kamchatka are known, were in the past avid consumers of the psychedelic mushroom *Amanita muscaria*, also known as *Fly agaric*. R. Gordon Wasson described in great detail the effects of this mushroom on the natives of Siberia and Kamchatka in his book *Soma: Divine Mushroom of Immortality*. The mushroom is intoxicating, and appeared to boost endurance of the natives, who would, for example, run faster and for longer distances after their sleds on snow. The shamans used mushrooms in order to experience visions that allowed them to see more deeply into the psyche of their patients and the spirit world. Such practices persisted since times immemorial among Siberian and Far Eastern natives. No harmful effects were observed or reported. Even deer were seen to be fond of the mushroom, which they were observed eagerly drinking the urine, containing a residue of the mushroom, whenever their riders would stop to relieve themselves.

When vodka was introduced, the native tribes in Siberia and the Far East were devastated by it. Vodka had also caused such excessive mortality and disease among the general population of the Soviet Union that one of the first reforms that Mikhail Gorbachev introduced when he came to power was to restrict the sale and production of alcohol. However, the economic damage from this reform (sales of alcohol being traditionally an important element in the Russian economy) and the resistance of the population were such that the reform was hastily abandoned.

Dr Belkin thought that it might be a good experiment to restrict supplies of vodka to an isolated population in one of the villages on Kamchatka and provide them instead with their trusty mushroom. When he mentioned this idea, half-seriously, half-jokingly, to his superiors at the Institute (many of whom were members of the Communist Party), he was told to forget all about it if he did not want himself and the rest of the Institute staff to be sent to a prison camp in Siberia.

There was another personal connection to the *Amanita* mushroom for me. My maternal uncle, Mikhail Leshchin, who was an NKVD officer until his enforced retirement on the Kamchatka Peninsula, due to some incurable skin disease, healed himself with *Amanita* mushroom after spending some years with the natives. He has learned their lore and healing methods and became a prominent holistic health advocate who was lauded by the *Pravda* newspaper for his work. Unfortunately, towards the end of his life, he started mixing *Amanita* decoctions with vodka. A bitter and disillusioned Communist, he died crippled by alcohol and diabetes.

As I wrote the book it became clear that any fundamental action against drug and alcohol addiction would polarize societies in a most fundamental way and would expose the hidden violence of the state against the individual, and of state against state through the institution of war. Any individual who fought addiction of the ruling elite to power, violence and corruption would become a traitor and a fugitive with few places to hide.

However, busking in the warm Californian sun and submerged in the sulfur-infused hot springs at the Esalen Institute, we forgot about the dire Soviet realities and gave vent to our fantasy. We speculated what would have happened if the idea of replacing vodka with a plant decoction was actually accepted and implemented throughout the Soviet Union (and maybe the world!).

Now, 30 or so years later, the governments around the world are proclaiming that the "War on Drugs" has been lost and are considering decriminalization and possible legalization of many drugs. The Big Pharma and independent researchers are looking for a recipe for a "happy pill" that would be an alternative to illegal drugs and some dangerous prescription drugs, as well as to tobacco and alcohol. Internet and retail sales of plant based recreational drugs are growing exponentially. But the current strategy in most countries is to still "put the ambulance down in the valley" to catch hundreds of thousands of human victims that fall from the drug cliff.

The Ambulance Down in the Valley

'Twas a dangerous cliff, as they freely confessed,

Though to walk near its crest was so pleasant;

But over its terrible edge there had slipped

A duke and full many a peasant.

So the people said something would have to be done,

But their projects did not at all tally;

Some said, "Put a fence 'round the edge of the cliff,"

Some, "An ambulance down in the valley..."

But the sensible few, who are practical too,

Will not bear with such nonsense much longer;

They believe that prevention is better than cure,

And their party will soon be the stronger.

Encourage them then, with your purse, voice, and pen,

And while other philanthropists dally,

They will scorn all pretence, and put up a stout fence

On the cliff that hangs over the valley.

Better guide well the young than reclaim them when old,

For the voice of true wisdom is calling.

"To rescue the fallen is good, but 'tis best

To prevent other people from falling."

Better close up the source of temptation and crime

Than deliver from dungeon or galley;

Better put a strong fence 'round the top of the cliff

Than an ambulance down in the valley.

Destination Unknown

July 15, 1976, Miami Courier.

A Pan American Boeing 707 en-route to London has disappeared over the ill-famed Bermuda triangle. No trace of the aircraft or its passengers has been found so far. Mr Jeremy Tripe, a controversial Los Angeles authority on the Bermuda triangle, has claimed that the latest incident conforms to the usual pattern and is yet further proof of his "time-space warp" hypothesis. However, the Soviet government newspaper "Izvestia", covering the same incident, has published an article by a Soviet scientist explaining the phenomenon on the basis of a magnetic anomaly caused by the peculiar position of the Sun and Moon in relation to the Earth at the time of the disappearances.

"Anna Charman... Nice name... What I can't understand is why she hasn't heard of the PVC controversy at the Goodrich plant?" Richard glanced over at his neighbour, unable to stop his appreciative gaze hover on the spot where her thighs emerged from beneath a chequered skirt. "Everybody I know in Cleveland has heard of it. But then..." he paused to sip his whiskey and rye, "but then..." Richard was distracted by the feeling of tingling warmth the whiskey gave him. He was not thinking at all clearly, and forgot what he was about to ask her next. Was it something about her job as a private secretary for... what was the name of the company she had mentioned?

"And what do you do for a living?" She showed a sudden willingness to take the lead in their flagging conversation.

Snowden was about to make one of his usual wisecracks about his occupation, saying he was either an alchemist or a village idiot, or both, but the voice from the loudspeaker interrupted him.

"We are now flying at a height of 30,000 feet, at an average speed of 560 miles per hour. We will shortly be flying over the Bermuda Islands. We are flying on schedule and should arrive in London soon after 11 o'clock tonight. Thank you."

"Oh, yes," Snowden was glad to have found an interesting topic of conversation. "Do you know that we are flying over the so-called 'Bermuda Triangle'?"

Miss Charman looked at him blandly and did not appear impressed by this revelation.

"Surely you've heard of it?" Snowden turned towards her, nearly upsetting his drink in the process.

She put her hands out, trying to cover her skirt.

"I'm sorry but I don't know what you are talking about." Her voice had lost whatever friendliness it had possessed a minute before. "And please be a bit more careful. I'd hate to have my skirt soaked in alcohol."

An uneasy silence ensued. Richard was disarmed by her sudden brusqueness. He knew he had bungled it with his attractive neighbor. He hated himself in these moments, when he was being too earnest, or showing enthusiasm for trivia. He decided to play the cool and analytical observer from now on, seeing that she had decided to turn off her initial charm.

He observed how Anna, for the third time in the last half an hour, had raised herself from her seat to look over her shoulder towards the back of the plane. "What the hell is she jumping up and down for all the time? If she has friends in the back, she should have sat with them," a sudden resentful thought came as a surprise to him.

"Sorry to disturb you." Her tone was still a touch abrupt, but it lacked the unfriendliness of a few minutes before. She must have forgiven him the nearly spilled drink. "I have to get out for a minute." She brushed past him, taking her black leather handbag with her.

Snowden looked absentmindedly through the now unobstructed window, where cotton-like tufts of clouds hung motionless over the sapphire-blue ocean. "It must be heaven down on Bermuda's white beaches," he thought wistfully, emptying his glass.

His eyes caught the reflection of the familiar plaid skirt. He shifted his legs to one side but, to his surprise, the skirt moved past him. He saw Anna nudge her way past an air-hostess who was serving drinks at the front of the plane. Two men followed her. Richard noticed how one man who had Asiatic features, and a broad, almost square frame, kept looking back over his shoulder. The other man, whom Richard hardly noticed at first, followed them towards the cockpit. The Asiatic-looking man whispered something in the hostess' ear. With a startled expression, she spilled the contents of the glass she was holding.

By this time Richard Snowden was beginning to feel uneasy. He knew enough about airplane hijackings to recognize the tell-tale signs. He had once served as an adviser on a team at the Hudson Institute, where his job was to analyze typical cases of air-piracy and possible ways of preventing them. It seemed that fate was providing him with an entirely unwanted opportunity for field study. Richard felt himself sobering up.

The hostess looked at the rows of passengers, unable to make a move, as the two men disappeared behind the greenish curtain that covered the entrance to the flight deck.

Richard saw Anna move swiftly to stand in front of the curtain, her legs slightly apart; her right hand nestled in her leather bag, her long dark hair swaying on her shoulders as she scanned the plane. For a moment, their eyes met, but she did not show any sign of recognition. Her face was animated, alive, and, he had to confess, even more attractive than before. The tension and the vacant expression that he had found so discomforting had vanished.

There was a jolt, as if the plane had hit an air pocket, and a few seconds later, the noise of the engines grew louder. The plane had picked up speed. Anna too seemed to have noticed the change and, diverting her eyes from the rows of passengers, looked back. At that very moment, a man on a seat a few feet from Richard's lunged towards her, knocking the hostess out of his way. The hostess screamed as she toppled over onto one of the passengers. In the confusion it was difficult for Richard to make out exactly what happened. The man, still a few feet away from where Anna was standing, reeled back abruptly and slumped to the ground. There was no noise of a shot, not even the slightest "pop". Anna's hand was inside her bag when Richard caught sight of her again.

Richard, who preferred to fight the imaginary battles, not the real ones, took heed of the fate of the hapless attacker. He took out his pen and wrote neatly on a piece of paper, which he tore out of his notebook, in his usual miniscule but clear handwriting: "July 15, 1976, Pan Am Flight 877 to London hijacked by three unidentified persons. The pattern of operation and especially the weapons indicate a highly organized operation." He then turned the notebook face down on the tray table.

There was a din of alarmed voices coming from the first class section as passengers stood up in their seats trying to see what was happening. The second-class passengers were still mostly unaware of what was going on. The loudspeaker clicked on and a voice with a heavy foreign accent announced: "Ladies and gentlemen, this plane is being diverted to another destination. If you maintain calm and order, we guarantee the safety of the passengers and crew. Any attempts to interfere with our actions will harm not only you, but the lives of other passengers as well. Please remain seated and obey instructions from our personnel, positioned at front, middle, and rear of the plane. Thank you."

The loudspeaker went dead and the hubbub in the plane temporarily subsided. People looked at each other in shock and disbelief. A child began to cry. Its mother tried to pacify it in loud whispers.

Richard turned his notebook over and corrected "three unidentified people" to "five unidentified people."

He glanced at the limp figure lying in the passageway. His guess was that the brave defender had been hit by some kind of hypodermic bullet carrying a quick-acting curare-type substance, which may have also been used to disable the pilots. The man's face was white and rigid, and his tongue was protruding slightly. Only now did Richard notice a switchblade knife, about three inches long, which the man was still clutching in his right hand.

"Poor bastard," thought Richard, feeling sorry for the man. He wondered who the man was. Probably an ex-policeman or soldier, or maybe even a criminal. Richard looked back down the plane, trying not to stick his head out too far. He caught a glimpse of a tall bearded man standing in the middle of the plane, his right hand hidden under the flap of his jacket.

A stern female voice rang out loudly: "Gentleman in the blue shirt. Please remain seated. If anyone wishes to use the rest room, you can do so one at a time, by lifting your hands in the air."

"Just like at a blessed kindergarten," Richard sneered to himself. She had certainly forgotten his name quickly. Now he was just a "gentleman in the blue shirt."

He tried to observe the other passengers. An overdressed lady with an elaborate hairdo in one of the front seats — someone had told him in the departure lounge that she was once a famous singer and a film star, now past her prime — was attempting to initiate a conversation with Anna, without much success. All Richard heard was an abrupt command to, "Please remain seated and be quiet." The actress kept fidgeting in her seat, whispering something animatedly to her neighbor, a stout man with a frightened look behind his glasses.

And then there was the Indian guru. "This could be interesting," Richard mused, glancing at the frail figure of a robed monk in a seat across the passage. He had always wanted to know how one of these "enlightened ones" would behave in extreme danger. Would all their tranquility and detachment fly out the window?

At that very moment, the Indian picked up a copy of *Time* magazine and began reading it, fondling a leaf with his free hand. "Hmmm, how tranquil!" Richard scoffed to himself, with a slight touch of envy. "A strange magazine for a guru to read! He'd look much better with a copy of the Bhagavad-Gita or the Upanishads. O tempora! O mores!... Oh well, at least he's not praying, or chewing his beads from fear."

The curtain at the front of the plane drew open and "the Mongol", as Richard baptized the first hijacker, appeared from behind it. His narrowly slit eyes scanned the plane, resting for a moment on the body lying in the passage. He exchanged a few inaudible words with his accomplice, and then moved decisively towards the body. Even though the man must have weighed a good 200 pounds, he picked him up without any visible effort and carried him towards an empty seat across the aisle from Richard's. Seeing the terrified face of the elderly woman cowering in the next seat, he turned around, silently commanding Richard to move over, and dumped the body next to him.

The man's head landed right on Richard's shoulder. Richard cringed but did not move. All he could do was to shove the head away and moved further into the corner. The hijacker's eyes narrowed: "He no dead. He asleep. In two hours give some vodka." He smiled derisively seeing Richard's fearful reaction.

The Mongol turned around, and his broad back disappeared again behind the curtain. Richard looked at the body next to him. It appeared lifeless, except for a trickle of saliva forming in the corner of the mouth. One eyelid was slightly open, the white of the eye showing. There was hardly any sign of breathing.

Richard felt sick. He was reminded of the car accident that happened years ago in Colorado. He had just turned twenty-five and was driving with his girlfriend to spend the weekend at her father's mountain cottage. Carelessly, he had taken the steering wheel from her to let her light a cigarette. They were on a rough mountain road, and he tried to steer around a small boulder that had rolled off the bank. He must have done it too quickly, or maybe they hit an icy patch, he never knew. The car spun out of control, hit the embankment, and rolled.

When he regained consciousness, his girlfriend's head was lying against his chest, the rest of her body trapped in the mangled interior of the car. What made him sick now was the memory of her unmoving body, the warm trickle of blood coming out of her mouth. It took the rescue team almost an hour to free them. He got away with some minor spinal injuries and a broken kneecap. He remembered seeing his girlfriend's body being loaded into the waiting ambulance.

In theory, life and death were routine in his line of work. If one could only total the number of virtual people he had sent into oblivion by a casual click of the mouse. Richard had become inured to such terms as "permissible megadeaths", "megamillion", "mutual assured destruction" (MAD for short), "selective counterforce strike" (which meant destruction of entire cities), and others, no less menacing. But these millions of "destroyed lives" were only numbers fed into his insatiable computers, mere ciphers in the equations he juggled to produce a neat, strategically plausible solution. Of course, in some remote and long-repressed corner of his mind he knew that these equations were somehow connected to the real world, to huge underground silos, to cataclysmic explosions, and to well-drilled military personnel with fingers on sensitive triggers. But it was easier to "think the unthinkable" than to feel the presence of a single human body, lying lifelessly right next to you. Even during the car crash, despite the shock, Richard had been struck, in a strange moment of detachment, by the sight of the frailty of the human body impacted by the well-formed, hardened, and so comfortable to ride in, metal frame of the car.

There was some disturbance at the back of the plane. Someone was crying hysterically. Heads were turning, and a few people, despite the warnings, were rising from their seats to see what was happening. Panic and agitation seemed to be growing.

It must have been close to an hour since the plane was hijacked, yet nobody knew the reason for the diversion of the aircraft, or who the hijackers were, or where the plane was headed. The hijackers were shouting orders, trying to calm everyone down, but with little success. A man sitting next to a woman who was sobbing hysterically rose and attempted to approach one of the hijackers, pleading with him to help her. He came within four or five feet of the man before being felled by the same noiseless weapon. A confused clamor of voices rose from the seats:

"Oh, God!"

"What's going to happen to us?"

"Brutes!... Criminals!"

Richard was trying to ignore the commotion. He knew it was pointless trying to interfere. He was looking out of the window so as not to look at the lifeless figure next to him. There was another reason, too. Twice during the past half hour, he had seen a military jet streak past them. He could not see any identifying marks. The type of plane was unfamiliar. He would have recognized it more readily if it was an American plane, or a plane from one of the NATO countries. Who could the plane belong to? It certainly looked like a fast, sophisticated aircraft. For a moment, it occurred to Richard that it might be a Russian MIG. Richard glanced furtively at the limp body next to him and snatched the notebook that he had left on the table in front of it. His hand was a little uneven as he wrote:

"The passengers are becoming panicky and uncontrollable. Two people rendered unconscious by the hijackers. They may have to knock out a lot of people as both the hijackers and the passengers may be getting out of control."

He glanced out of the window and added: "An unidentified military aircraft, possibly a MIG, appears to be following our plane."

Anna stuck her head out from behind the curtain separating the passenger compartment from the flight deck and shouted something. After a few seconds, The Mongol appeared. He stood there silently, summing up the situation. The hubbub was reaching deafening proportions. His eyes searched the plane for some sort of solution and fixed on the overdressed actress, who squirmed under his heavy gaze.

"You," he bellowed, pointing at her with a crooked finger sporting a largish gold ring. "I order! Do something... dance, sing, do striptease... I order!"

The actress appeared shocked. He pulled her from her seat roughly, stood her in the middle of the passageway, and repeated in a loud hiss, which left little doubt about the fact that he meant business: "You obey, or you die."

Shocked and confused, she attempted an ingratiating smile.
"Something happy?"
"Anything!"
Her hand groped the air for a non-existent microphone, and then she smoothed her dress a little nervously and began in a raspy nightclub alto:

> "Those magnificent men,
> In their flying machines..."

"Louder, louder," prompted The Mongol.

Her voice penetrated the din and even people at the rear of the plane exchanged glances and stretched their necks to see where the song was coming from. The hubbub gradually began to die down.

A minute later, while the song was still ringing in the air, a voice came over the loudspeaker: "Ladies and gentlemen, we ask you to maintain calm and order. We guarantee your safety if you obey our instructions. The hostesses will now serve drinks, free of charge. You can also ask for free cigarettes and souvenirs from the plane's shop." The voice of the announcer was replaced by soft music.

The hostesses, first nervously, then more and more confidently, began handing out drinks and cigarettes.

An irate voice asked a hostess: "Who are they, anyway?"

The hostess shrugged her shoulders. "Just sit quietly and listen to the announcements. There is nothing we can do right now." Gradually the atmosphere in the plane became almost normal. The hostesses were doing brisk business.

Richard could not help but admire the skill with which the hijackers had handled the emergency. The actress returned to her seat, looking flushed and excited. The holy man was now talking quietly to his neighbor, a dark-skinned young man in his early twenties, his traveling companion. Richard strained to hear.

"Do you think they are going to kill us?" the young man was asking.

"Remember the words of Lord Krishna," intoned the guru. "No one can get killed or kill anyone. It is just the unfolding of the karma."

"Yes, I know, but can we do something real quick to change the karma?" the young man insisted with some urgency.

"Take your eyes off that hostess' blouse and meditate," the guru intoned. "Then at least you will not have to go through a similar incident in your next life."

"Here they go," thought Richard. "They'll go on blathering about their karma and future lives even while they are being deprived of the present one."

The next few hours passed relatively peacefully. A few of the passengers got roaring drunk, making full use of the free offer. A respectable-looking English matron ordered two cartons of *Benson & Hedges* cigarettes, "...one for my husband, who is going to meet me at Heathrow, and one for my brother."

A female passenger tried to initiate a conversation with one of the hijackers. One tipsy man jokingly offered chocolate to Anna. She affected a rather strained smile, and refused.

When darkness fell, most people fell asleep, worn out. A man behind Richard hiccupped incessantly. Richard was about to doze off himself when he heard the engines slow down. The lights went off, except for a few soft lights along the luggage rack. The plane was changing altitude. Richard heard a droning noise. He looked through the window. Outside was nothing but impenetrable darkness.

Finally, the plane touched down. Richard saw the lights on the runway go off immediately after the plane came to a standstill. He scribbled down:

"The plane has landed at an unidentified airfield. No lights or other planes visible."

The engines died and the hijackers emerged from the cockpit. As they drew the curtain open, Richard distinguished the bodies of the pilot and the co-pilot lying in a formless heap by the entrance to the cockpit. It suddenly dawned on him: the two hijackers had been piloting the plane all these hours and managed to bring it to land safely! These were no ordinary terrorists.

But the greatest surprise was yet to come. As the two men passed him, they stopped at the seat where the Indian holy man was sitting and indicated to him that he was to follow them. The Indian attempted to exchange some parting remarks with his companion but was led away.

The rear exit opened, and the strange trio disembarked. Two refueling vehicles pulled up. Almost simultaneously, Richard heard the loud stamping of feet on the gangway and saw paratroopers with parachute packs on their backs running onto the plane. They occupied positions all along the passage and stood poised, mute and unsmiling. Their khaki uniforms bore no insignia.

Most of the passengers were now awake. Richard saw a paratrooper unceremoniously shove a rifle butt into the stomach of a complaining passenger who attempted to get up from his seat. Not a word was uttered. There were no longer any reassurances of safety. The passengers were treated like cattle on the way to the slaughterhouse.

Richard felt sick in the stomach. He was going to die ingloriously just like his girlfriend, a victim of some terrible mistake of which he was a chance victim.

Although morning was coming, it was still quite dark inside the plane. He now had no doubt that the man next to him was dead. With a tremendous effort of will, he scribbled another entry in his diary:

"The plane boarded by paratroopers with no identifying insignia. An Indian holy man was the only passenger taken off by the hijackers. The plane is being refueled. Destination unknown."

He rolled the paper tightly, inserted it into a small empty whiskey bottle on his tray and screwed the top on firmly. It was the only rational act he could think of. He wanted to leave at least a few clues. As soon as he sealed the bottle, he felt himself gripped by ugly, naked fear.

Anna was coming down the passageway, about to leave the plane. As she was passing a paratrooper not far from Richard, she bumped into him, and said, almost inaudibly,

"Izvinitye." That was Russian! She had said, "Sorry." It was one of the few words that had stuck in his memory from the crash course in Russian he took when they hired him at Hudson.

One thing Richard knew for certain: he did not want to die, not in this way. He beckoned to Anna as she was passing him: "Remember me? My name is Richard Snowden. I am involved in top-secret work for the American government. I may be useful to you!"

She looked at him, but without a trace of recognition or familiarity and passed by without saying a word.

The refueling trucks were being driven away. Two more men in paratrooper uniforms, equipped with parachute packs, walked rapidly towards the front of the plane and disappeared into the cockpit. After a minute or two, the engines restarted.

Richard glanced at the face of the body next to him and recoiled in horror. The face of the man who had seemed dead a minute ago was contorted into a wide, empty smile, and his eyes were wide open! Richard felt a warm sensation along his legs. His bladder had involuntarily emptied. He almost passed out.

His name was being called: "Snowden!... Snowden!"

He lifted his eyes. Was he dreaming? But it was The Mongol, standing above him, shaking him by the shoulder.

"Come, quick," he urged.

Richard forced himself to get up and tried to edge past the body next to him without touching it. The Mongol prodded him impatiently. Dazed, Richard walked down the tarmac straight into the open door of a waiting van.

There were other people inside, conversing in what Richard now definitely recognized as Russian. Faces appeared out of the darkness in front of him, looking at him with detached curiosity. Someone laughed, pointing at his wet pants and saying something incomprehensible but, Richard was sure, terribly rude, in Russian. He felt an acute sense of humiliation. There was a person sitting on each side of him on the rough, wooden benches. He felt the closeness of their warm, muscular bodies, and a smell of perspiration and strong tobacco. He had a feeling of claustrophobia. He attempted to move away, saying, "I won't run away, I promise you."

The men moved even closer, and each of them, as if on command, held Richard's arms. He struggled in vain to free himself from their grip. Another face appeared in front of him. It was The Mongol again, who patted him on the arm. Richard felt a sharp prick and almost immediately voices around him began to sound muted, swallowed by a brilliant cloud, which, in Richard's dimming consciousness, somehow transformed itself into a large, sweetly smelling onion. When the cloud dispersed, there was dark nothingness.

Win Some, Lose Some

When Richard finally awoke, he was lying on a thin mattress that seemed to have been designed by an acupuncturist. He was staring up at the shiny interconnected springs and hooks of the base of an upper bunk. He did not know how long he had been lying like this, with his eyes wide open, studying the regular shapes formed by the wire. Next, he became aware of a steady hum permeating the room.

Out of the corner of his eye, he saw another double bunk bed. On the bottom bunk sat an Indian monk, cross-legged, with long grey hair interspersed with black streaks and dark, smooth skin, smiling at him. Richard closed his eyes tightly, trying to expel the vision from his consciousness. He must be hallucinating.

As he struggled to regain his mental faculties, memories of the previous night began to filter through, piece by piece. A tentative question formed itself in his mind: "Where am I and what happened to the rest of the passengers?"

He was not sure whether it was just a thought or something he had said aloud. It must have been the latter; for the Indian replied in a high-pitched voice, which Richard found slightly grating on his sensitive ears: "We are aboard a Russian submarine. I cannot tell you why we are here. For the last few hours you have been lying in bed, unconscious."

"Russian? Submarine?" It took Richard a few more minutes before the pieces of the jigsaw puzzle began to fit together. "And I presume we are on a cruise to the North Pole?" he joked lamely.

The Indian was silent.

"What's your name?" asked Richard.

"My name?" the Indian hesitated for a moment. "One of these Russian officers who speak good English keeps calling me 'Swami'. I guess it is as good a name as any other."

Richard felt irritated again. Why can't these Indian fellows ever give you a straight answer?

The door of their compartment opened and a Navy officer came in. Behind the officer, Richard glimpsed the figure of a sailor with a submachine gun. "Marvelous, isn't it," he thought. "As if we are going to escape from a submarine."

"Gentlemen," the officer's English was quite passable, "would you like to have your lunch now?"

Richard looked at his watch. It was nearly midday. Was it the same day they had left the plane?

He could not be sure even of that. They must have given him a hell of a knockout drug. He rubbed his temples, trying to ease the throbbing pain.

"What would you like, gentlemen?" continued the officer politely.

"I want a stiff whiskey to knock this crap out of my head and maybe some sandwiches and a bowl of hot soup," said Richard.

"And you, Swami?"

"And I want a glass of stiff tomato juice and maybe some nuts and fruit if you have them."

The officer smiled at Swami's lighthearted jibe. Richard pointedly ignored it. He did not think the situation was funny.

"Yes, we have supplies of fresh fruit and nuts on board especially for you. We gathered that the sailor's fare might not be the most suitable for you. We have fresh pears, avocados, and... coconut juice. The tomatoes for your juice come from our own hydroponic mini-garden aboard the submarine."

"How very thoughtful of you," said Swami, without the slightest touch of sarcasm.

"Anything else I can do for you, gentlemen?" The officer was politeness itself. "There are English books and magazines on the shelf, and a few board games. Your lunch should be served in about an hour, as soon as we are finished with the crew."

After lunch, Richard walked over to the bookshelf. The only recent periodical was the English language version of a glossy magazine called *Sputnik* — the Russian answer to Reader's Digest. There were some back copies of the left-wing *Ramparts*, a few issues of the radical left magazine *New Times,* and a complete collection of last year's *Navy International*.

Richard sighed. This was not going to be an exciting journey. He badly needed something to distract himself from his headache and worries about the future. He glanced at the bookshelf with board games on it.

"Do you play chess, Swami?"

"No, I have never played before, but if you show me how to, I would be glad to be your companion."

Richard felt dejected. He was one of the best chess players in their think tank. It would take weeks before Swami's game could become even remotely interesting. But what else was there to do aboard a submarine that was spinning the bottom of the ocean towards some Russian hell-hole?

He showed Swami the moves and played one practice game.

"Are you ready to play?" he asked. Swami wanted to practice on his own for a few minutes. Finally, he declared, "I like this game. There is an infinite number of possibilities, but only some are..." he hesitated, looking for the right expression, "more pleasing to the mind than others."

"Strictly speaking," interjected Richard, "the possibilities aren't infinite. There are only 10 to the power of 10, to the power of 50 possible games of chess. But the exact prediction of moves is certainly beyond not only the human brain — it will be beyond computers thousands of times more powerful than present ones. However, I do agree with you that some moves are more interesting or, as you say, more aesthetically pleasing than others."

"It also reminds me," continued the Indian, "of certain chapters from the Bhagavad-Gita. If you want to play the game of life or chess, you may have to sacrifice some of your pieces, especially if you know that they only go off the board temporarily, until the next game, meaning next life."

Richard simply wanted to get on with the game and ignored Swami's excursion into Hindu philosophy. He set out the pieces on the board. But the Indian continued, "This game seems to me to be a symbolic expression for the whole battle of life, with its opposing forces, plus the different capabilities of the pieces and their rules of behavior to guide them."

Richard had to admit that there was actually some truth in what the Indian was saying. Chess was the strategist's favorite game at Hudson. He remembered reading a theory that chess had begun its history in India as the world's first war game, and, at the same time, a game heavily laden with spiritual symbolism. So, it seemed — he almost chuckled aloud — that the life philosophy of this Hindu mystic was not so vastly different from the one adopted at the Hudson Institute. As far as he could see, in both cases sacrifices were thought to be necessary for the sake of a neat strategic solution and the final victory.

Swami chose to play white and Richard motioned him to start first. Richard did not bother to tell him anything about the various opening strategies. He expected him to make some drastic mistakes but decided to respond to them on their own merit, forgetting the more traditional moves and counter-moves.

To his surprise, Swami's first moves approximated very closely to what was known as the "Old Indian defence." It appeared that Swami had intuitively grasped the idea that it was not necessary to occupy the center of the board, as most novices think, in order to exert pressure on the king from the side. Of course, Richard could not be sure whether the Indian really understood what he was doing.

"Ha!" Richard forgot for a moment that he was playing a complete beginner. "This looks very much like something that Misha Tal would have done, unable to resist challenging the opponent with his rooks." He was becoming engrossed in the game. "Now I'll show him he can't get away with it." He moved one of his pawns forward; he was endangering Swami's attacking bishops that were trying to destroy his king's defence. He leant back in his chair to admire the position of the pieces.

"You see," he said with a slight air of superiority, "it is advisable to envisage the consequences of one's moves a few steps ahead."

"This is exactly what I am trying to do," replied Swami, moving his rook one square.

"What is he up to?" mused Richard, "Make me a present of his Knight?" He paused for a second, as he always did before taking a piece, no matter how straightforward the move looked.

Suddenly, he saw it. All the Indian had to do was to move his Queen to F4 to have him checkmated. How careless of him! But then, surely the Indian had not planned it that way. It would be simply too much to expect from a novice.

Defending his King against this anticipated move entailed not only letting Swami's Knight get away, but also a complex rearrangement of his entire strategy. He decided to risk it and take the Knight. Surely Swami did not foresee the fatal move.

Swami's hand hovered over the board... and then moved the Queen to F4. "What do you call this again?" he asked innocently, after a couple more moves that Richard could not neutralize in time.

"Checkmate," blurted Richard, furious with himself. Now this little Indian nutcase is going to imagine that he is the greatest chess player in the world! He could have easily prevented the checkmate had he not underestimated his opponent so greatly. He certainly would not do that again.

He wanted to play another game right away, but decided to lie down and rest first. He forgot to thank Swami for the game. As he was walking towards his bed, he heard Swami say, "One only wins, in chess or life, if one does not get involved with the business of winning or losing. You wanted my Knight, and that was your downfall. Similarly, desire, though perfectly natural, is the cause of all tragedy in life. But one cannot pretend to be without desire if one is only a pawn who dreams of becoming a Queen. To be free of desire, one must elevate oneself to the status of the Cosmic Chess Player, the omnipotent Grand Master. Sacrificing one's pieces to reach one's own ends is nothing but a rationalized murder."

Richard's temples throbbed so badly after Swami's harangue that he felt like whacking him on the head with the chessboard.

"I am sure, Swami," he said, trying not to lose his temper, "that what you have just said has some profound meaning, but right now it somehow escapes me. Besides, my head is aching horribly, and I need some sleep."

"Headache?" queried Swami. "Let your attention stay at the point where it aches, effortlessly. Then, as you breathe into your diaphragm, say in your mind, 'Vee,' and as you breathe into your chest say 'Naab,' and as you breathe out say 'Ohm'. The pain will soon pass away."

It was the biggest piece of nonsense Richard had ever heard. He thought he ought to ask for some Panadol, or its Russian equivalent of it at any rate. But he felt too listless to do even that. His head was hurting badly. What did he have to lose? He began half-heartedly murmuring to himself, slowly breathing in and out, "Vee, Naab, Ohm, Vee, Naab,

Ohm..." Gradually, his breathing slowed and became more even. In a minute or two, he was fast asleep.

When Richard woke up, his watch showed four o'clock — he could not figure out at first whether in the morning or afternoon. Swami was sitting on his bunk in his usual cross-legged position, writing something on a pad of paper perched on his knee. It must have been four o'clock in the morning, for Richard felt much fresher. He must have been asleep for a long time. His head felt much clearer.

Swami noticed that Richard was awake. "Good morning, I saved some oranges and nuts for you."

"Thank you."

Richard felt almost genuinely grateful for losing the headache after Swami's trick. He remembered the chess game they had played.

It seemed funny to him now that he had gotten so upset over the game. He knew he could beat the man any time he wanted to. But he certainly had picked the game up fast, he thought. In fact, Richard had to concede that he had never seen anyone pick up something as complicated as a game of chess so fast.

Swami moved the paper away.

"I guess we should introduce ourselves properly." Richard stretched out his hand, "Richard Snowden, I am a US citizen and a consultant."

"You already know what to call me. My real name is not important." Swami's quick smile bared a row of white, faultless teeth. "As to the kind of job I do, until yesterday I was the spiritual head of an organization with branches in many countries, spreading a certain meditation technique. Today I do not know what my job is," he chuckled innocently. "But today, as yesterday, I am nothing but a reflection of a changeless Brahman upon the eternally changing mirror of time and space..."

Richard remembered now. He had seen photographs of the man a few years ago, splashed across pages of glossy magazines and daily papers, heralding yet another fashionable "spiritual revival." Inevitably, there was some sort of scandal or gossip attached to the story, involving either a movie star or a pop group, he had forgotten which.

"And what do you think the Russians want from you?" Richard asked.

"Perhaps they want me to collaborate on the Russian translation of The Bhagavad-Gita," joked Swami. "Ironically enough, I always used to say that when the Russians get interested in meditation, they will do it in a big way. I did not realize that they would go to quite such lengths..." He chuckled again. "Lovely oranges, won't you have one?" He handed Richard an orange wrapped up in a crumpled napkin.

Ten or so days had passed more or less uneventfully since they moved aboard the submarine. Richard began to lose track of time. Swami worked diligently on his new interpretation of the six systems of Indian philosophy, which, he said, he had been too busy to do in his days as a popular guru. Richard was amazed at his productivity. He worked on average 18 hours a day, and even when Richard occasionally caught him with his eyes closed, he could not be sure whether the Indian was asleep, meditating, or simply resting.

They played one or two games of chess every day, with Richard losing about half of them towards the end. But this was no longer upsetting him. He realized that behind Swami's child-like simplicity was one of the most cunning and calculating minds he had ever encountered. The spiritual analogies and quips with which Swami accompanied the games did not irk him nearly quite as much as before. He realized that it allowed him to learn a great deal about Hindu philosophy, painlessly.

Finally, the journey came to an end.

"Where did they find it?" The Director wanted to know.

"About 450 miles North-East of Barbados," the Colonel answered, checking his notes. "It was picked up by one of our fishing boats and handed over to the Coast Guard. They couldn't make head nor tail of it, thought it was some kind of hoax."

"They could be right, you know." The Director sounded unconvinced.

"Of course, we can't be absolutely sure that it was from the missing plane," the Colonel was trying to be deferential to his superior's skepticism. "But the location, the currents, and all the other details seem to fit surprisingly well. Our experts confirm that the handwriting is definitely Snowden's. Also, our intelligence reports indicate that very recently, someone — maybe not Snowden, but any other explanation would be a terrific coincidence — has given the Russians a lot of information about the research we've commissioned at the Hudson."

"OK. I can see that. But what I find suspicious is this part about the Indian holy man. How do you fit him into the intelligence picture?"

"I must agree with you, Sir," said the Colonel; "we also find it rather puzzling. By the way, we tracked one Soviet nuclear sub near the place where the plane's wreckage was found and another one off the African coast, moving steadily up north. "

"Look," the Director deliberated for a few seconds, "if you are sure that this report is not a clever forgery or a concoction of some maniac, you'd better give it all your attention from now on. If the Russians were really involved in the disappearance of that plane — and the subsequent death of its passengers   — they must have been after something really big. Bigger than Snowden and the Indian. So we'd better make sure we are not missing something that is going to blow up right in our faces."

He paused for a moment, furrowing his brows.

"I want you to carry on with a preliminary investigation and, if anything significant turns up, give it top priority. You can have men from Division S4 to help you. If you think the results justify the need for more money and people, come and see me straight away. And you'd better read this too. There is something really fishy going on here."

Before waving the Colonel away he gave him a thick file entitled "Soviet Naval and Air Bases on the African Continent."

The Supersoma

The First Secretary's voice was somber, almost solemn. "Comrades, we have before us a task of the highest priority. The entire future of our nation, even more, the future of world communism is at stake."

He looked around the conference table. The cream of the Soviet scientific elite was sitting before him. There was Dr Plushkov, the brilliant cybernetician, whose task was to apply computer science to social control. State-wide personal data banks and the moneyless distribution of goods and services were two of his recent projects. However, he was not able to get them off the ground due to a lack of suitable computers and trained personnel. It seemed unfortunate that, to have the means to engineer a smoothly-run society, you first needed to have a smoothly-run economy. But he was a scientist, not a politician, and scientists never lose hope easily, unless their grants run out.

Across from Dr Plushkov sat Dr Abosov, the famous surgeon who was now developing a method of behavior modification that was promising to bring the Party some very novel and effective tools. Next to him sat Drs Kon and Larchuk, experts on the latest methodologies in the field of brain/behavior control.

Next to the First Secretary (known among his close associates as Glavny, the Chief) sat Vlas Bur, the newly appointed Head of the top secret project named by the participating scientists, who tended to ignore political correctness, "Nirvana," which Glavny was about to reveal.

Vlas had no scientific background whatever, but nonetheless had been picked by Glavny to supervise the most sensitive project ever undertaken in the name of the Party. They had known each other since the war days and even before, since the days of the purges, when Vlas had rendered some of his most appreciated services to the State.

But there was more to it than mere personal friendship and well-tested loyalty.

Glavny knew very well that the top scientists whom he personally selected for the team might object to being supervised by a man who had been a cowherd for the first part of his life and a Party hack for the second. But he trusted Vlas more than he trusted these wily wordmongers who, he feared, might get him into an even bigger pickle than that into which one of his predecessors had landed himself with experiments as a result of corn and virgin lands. Vlas always got things done, whether it was purging the Party or organizing a research team. He had that acute peasant's intuition, which allowed him, as Glavny (who was not averse to an occasional scatological joke) used to say, to "separate the bull from the contents of its stomach."

Anyhow, he had appointed Vlas to head the team, and made him answerable to nobody but himself.

Glavny looked around the table from beneath his bushy eyebrows, resting his gaze momentarily on the face of each participant.

"Comrades, I think we have to be frank, at least among ourselves, and admit that we have reached a critical point in the development of our society. The lofty Communist ideals that have motivated our people during the preceding six decades have lost much of their appeal. As Marx might have said, the material and scientific basis of our society has changed much faster than the ideological superstructure.

"Crime, delinquency, social apathy, loafing on the job, general corruption and drunkenness — these are some of the symptoms of the growing gap between the material and the ideological, or, as some of you would no doubt prefer to say, psychological, or even moral — aspects of life. Frankly, I do not think we can go on much longer calling this social malaise the inheritance of the past. This explanation served its purpose during the first half century of our rule, but now has begun to sound a bit unconvincing.

"Alas, people are becoming more and more cynical. I was recently told of the existence of a joke, which, regretfully, has been enjoyed even by some Party members. The joke is that for the past twenty years, our country has been caught up in a transitional phase between socialism and communism. And do you know, comrades, what the name of that phase is — it is alcoholism. Yes, alcoholism!"

The members of the conference appeared duly shocked by this sacrilegious insinuation, even though some of them barely managed to suppress a smile. They knew the joke and recognized that it had more than a grain of truth in it.

"Which," Glavny surveyed the table again with the deep-seated eyes that made most people feel uneasy, "brings us to the subject matter of this meeting."

He took a big gulp from the glass of water in front of him. Those who knew Glavny intimately could not help but think that he secretly wished he had a different kind of liquid in the faceted crystal carafe in front of him. No one could doubt that when he spoke about alcoholism, he spoke from deep and profound personal experience.

Glavny cleared his throat and continued.

"As you know, alcoholism has become a major problem in Russia! I will be frank on this point — the revenue from the sale of alcohol has, in the past, paid for a goodly share of our Defence bill and mopped up people's excess purchasing power. It has also provided them with a legitimate outlet for energy that otherwise may have become socially disruptive. So, you may find me a bit old-fashioned, but I have always insisted, and still insist that there are not only bad, but also some good things to be said about alcohol."

There were some sympathetic nods and grunts from around the table, although Drs Kon and Larchuk remained stone-faced.

"But — and this is a big but — you have been reading, I presume, the classified report released on the incidence of alcoholism among our population, its effect on absenteeism and productivity, crime, delinquency, and longevity. It is clear from these statistics that we can't go on the way we are. Otherwise our society will simply disintegrate, buried under the rubble of empty bottles and beer cans. A goodly proportion of our adult population will end up either in prison or in a mental institution, sooner rather than later."

This was well-trodden ground and participants were waiting for Glavny to announce some sensational revelation to justify his invitation of such an illustrious panel and his own grandiloquent opening words.

"Our people's misguided and unmitigated indulgence," continued Glavny gravely, reading from a piece of paper, "this — what do you call it?... this wave of... hedonism? — has even brought to our shores a scourge we thought could only take firm hold on capitalist soil, I mean — hard and soft drugs. Despite penalties which are probably the toughest in the world, and which we intend to make even tougher, incidence of drug abuse, especially among the young, is rising.

"So, some of our scientific colleagues have spent the past few months working on possible solutions which would allow us, while there is still time, to reverse the present disastrous trends. However, here I am getting out of my depth, so I will hand you over to Dr Abosov who is more qualified to fill you in on the latest developments."

Dr Abosov, a tall man with a prominent nose, bald head, and thoughtful, sad eyes, spoke confidently, now and again glancing at his notes.

"Comrades, it's been a few months now since we began working in our research establishment at the Academy on the biocybernetic model of human behavior." Dr Abosov looked at Glavny apologetically as if to excuse himself for having to use big words.

"There are still things which are far from clear in our complex model, but we have made one important finding:

that the single, most effective way of changing human behavior and motivation is to affect the pleasure drive of the individual. The other alternatives involve even greater regimentation, social controls, and stricter punishments than we currently possess. It is true that we have perfected some of these methods, both in the laboratory and in the field, but the picture of the future society which relies exclusively on such negative and punitive measures is a rather unpleasant one to contemplate."

Dr Abosov glanced towards Glavny and Vlas as if anticipating their objections.

"I agree that there were times in the history of our country when such harsh methods were both necessary and justified. However, my colleagues and I believe that at the present stage of scientific development these methods are neither necessary nor desirable. We can achieve the same results through different means..."

"By what means?" Vlas intervened abruptly. "Could you please explain in practical terms what your alternatives are? I must confess that I fail to connect your ideas with what the First Secretary has just been saying about our alcohol and drugs problem."

"Well," Dr Abosov affected a forced smile, "if you want me to put it into plain, rather crude terms, we confirmed an age-old observation that human behavior is motivated primarily by the avoidance of pain and the pursuit of pleasure or, to put it graphically, by 'the stick and the carrot.' While in the past we used to rely predominantly upon the stick — the only carrot being an imaginary picture of the classless society towards which we are all striving — the time has come, I think, to change the emphasis to include a carrot."

Vlas put a deliberately puzzled look on his face and stretched out his arms, as if saying, "Show me your carrot."

"To come back to the words of our First Secretary, alcohol, even though it may appear to be a carrot to some people, is actually still part of the old stick. Its ultimate effects are depression, as well as mental and physical deterioration."

"Yes, we know that," Vlas interrupted him again. "So, what are your practical proposals?"

"Well," Dr Abosov coughed softly, "my colleague Dr Plushkov and his team have experimented with various forms of reinforcement, such as praise by fellow workers, better wages, and somewhat improved living conditions. We found that, while these have some effect, it is not profound or lasting. People become dissatisfied fast and asked for better goods and services, as well as higher wages."

Glavny was smiling broadly. "Pardon me, Doctor, but may I point out a rather simple fact? For a good many years, the capitalists have found that better wages and living conditions were enough of a carrot to keep the masses contented and, unfortunately, unresponsive to our calls for the world revolution. Why shouldn't we be so lucky?"

Dr Plushkov, a thick-set man with quick, elusive eyes and a slight stammer, intervened, as if to help and rescue his colleague.

"As we pointed out to you in our preliminary report, Comrade First Secretary, our computer model has shown us that we simply cannot match the standard of living obtainable in most developed Western countries... within the framework of our economy. It would demand such an increase in the production of consumer goods that the national defence and the heavy industries, which are essential for our broader goals, would simply collapse. We have played through various scenarios, such as greater reliance on profits and extensive computerization of industry, but still failed to produce the degree of efficiency which private enterprise in the West is somehow able to attain."

He paused briefly, coughed, and uttered something that could not be uttered at any other gathering but this.

"To put it quite bluntly, our only remaining alternatives are to convert our socialist economy into a free market one, or to risk dangerously weakening our defence by diverting large sums of money into agriculture, as well as the consumer and service industries."

"And we obviously can't do either, can we?" roared Glavny. "Not after all the years of sacrifice and struggles and deprivations that our people have endured. The socialist experiment cannot, must not be allowed to fail... Comrades," Glavny lowered his voice as only he could, suffusing it with a tone of both menace and supplication. "How will history judge us if we retreat now?" He looked around the room.

Everyone was busy looking at their notes.

"No, we obviously cannot retreat. This is why I said at the beginning that we are now faced with a great — and grave — historical responsibility. We have to find answers that are different from anything we have tried before."

Dr Abosov waited a few seconds respectfully before continuing with his report.

"Yes, Comrade First Secretary, we have experimented with other methods of satisfying the pleasure urge. We tried psychopharmacological means of reinforcement or, to put it bluntly, new types of pleasure-producing drugs. In our experiments we tried to correlate using drug-based reinforcement with productivity and other indicators of social usefulness. We found that, at least to a small degree, the idea works. We are now developing better and safer pharmacological reinforcements, in other words, better and safer drugs."

There was a noticeable hush in the room.

"You're not telling us," Vlas erupted in derisive laughter as soon as Dr Abosov finished his speech, "that the best alternative you could come up with was hooking people on 'happy' drugs to get them to work better? Look, any Chinaman could have told me that. And how do you think we are going to justify all this after calling narcotics a ploy of the bourgeoisie to dull the minds of the workers? This sounds to me like a completely hare-brained idea."

Dr Abosov was obviously stung by the remark. His face became red and his voice quivered slightly.

"Comrade Bur, we are scientists and, as such, concern ourselves not with ideological justifications but with scientific realities. Justifications are your specialty, and, if you will pardon me saying so, in the past you have successfully managed to justify things that were even harder to justify."

He now seemed to balance on a sort of high-roll that could make him either a hero — or a martyr.

"And, please, let us not misuse the word 'drug'," he continued. "Vitamins are drugs, you know, and so is aspirin. Any substance which is used in a controlled fashion towards a specific goal can be called a drug. We are developing a whole range of increasingly safer, non-addictive, and non-stupefying substances from psychoactive plants. Their mode of action is quite different from the street narcotics commonly used now, such as heroin, marijuana, LSD-25, and other minor and major psychedelics. The drugs we are developing belong to a newly discovered class of neurotransmitters. They activate the pleasure circuitry much more directly than any of the previously known substances and have fewer side-effects. They are also natural and plant-based, at least in their precursor form."

"So what do you call your new 'natural' drugs?" asked Vlas derisively, "'superdope'?"

There were chuckles and smiles around the room.

"At the Institute," Dr Abosov continued, ignoring the remark of his opponent, "we group these new psychotropic agents under the generic name 'Supersoma'. When we go public, we may want to use some more politically correct term such as 'Socialin,' or 'Communazine,' or something in that vein."

Glavny was sitting with his eyes closed, murmuring softly, almost to himself. "Well, we have borrowed their advertising and called it 'goods display,' their computers and called them 'electronic calculating machines,' what is to stop us from taking their drugs, improving them, and calling them 'Socialin'? In fact, as long as it does the job, and rescues us from this shithole, the name rather appeals to me."

Dr Abosov saw that his frankness and his powers of persuasion were having an effect.

"Tell me," Glavny broke out of his reverie, "how safe is your... Socialin? I don't want a bunch of stoneheads walking around Red Square."

Dr Abosov seemed happy that the discussion was finally taking a more constructive turn.

"We are in a bit of a predicament here, to speak the truth. We found that the more universally effective and powerful the substance, the greater its side effects. The best example is our Supersoma 187L. But we have also developed Supersoma XL-14 which is still quite effective, but is almost completely free of side effects. All it does is to occasionally cause the user to go into a fit of burping. I do not want to get too technical here, but this has something to do with overstimulation of the parasympathetic nervous system that the drug produces. But it has no effect on the workers' mind, bodies, or their productivity. "

"Sounds familiar to me," interjected Vlas. "The stronger the brew, the bigger the hangover. But I guess we can live with a moderately belching proletariat, as long as it keeps marching ahead towards the goal of Communism."

"This is why," continued Dr Abosov, ignoring Bur's remark that he did not find funny at all, "our colleagues working under the auspices (he almost said "cover") of the Institute for Comparative Physiology have also been looking into the possibility of activating the pleasure circuitry in the brain, but without recourse to drugs. And I am sure they will come up with a news scoop to report."

Dr Kon rose to speak. She was the granddaughter of a famous Russian physiologist, which had helped her to rise rapidly to the top of the scientific establishment. A plump woman in her forties, with a very plain, but not unintelligent face, she turned nervously towards Glavny, whom she was meeting for the first time.

"Our task of having to find an effective pleasure-producing technique which would involve neither drugs nor deep brain implants was complicated by the virtual absence of any hardcore scientific data on the subject, especially in our country."

She felt self-conscious about using scientific terminology in front of her audience, most of whom she knew were barely literate, but she continued reading from her prepared notes.

"Of course, there are many subjective reports and claims made on behalf of various religions and cults, purporting to provide the experience of so-called 'bliss' or 'nirvana'. We have looked at many of these approaches — Hindu, Buddhist, Tibetan, Kabbalistic, Christian, Shinto, Sufi, and their modern cult offshoots. After extensive analysis, facilitated by computer processing, we have picked out several elements that appear to be present in most of these techniques. On that basis, we have devised our own technique which incorporates the most important elements of the traditional approaches while leaving out the unnecessary mysticism and rituals."

Glavny nodded his head approvingly at the last sentence. Vlas was looking distracted.

"We have discovered," continued Dr Kon, "that our new technique does indeed produce a marked 'pleasure response,' but only in a few rare individuals whom we call the ST (for Spontaneous Transcender) type. In our research, they comprised a little less than 0.05% of the general population, excluding the temporal lobe epileptics who are rather prone to having these so-called 'mystical' experiences. The rest of our 'normal' population were able to experience some relaxation, but the degree of 'pleasure' was minimal and was mostly a result of autosuggestion."

"Are you saying that only five people out of every 10,000 could get something out of your new technique?" asked Vlas incredulously. He was aware that a large sum of money and a great deal of sophisticated equipment were tied up in the Institute's research.

Dr Larchuk, a tall, gaunt man with a nervous tick and a craggy, much wrinkled face, rose slightly from his chair, indicating that he wanted to speak. He had to rise in defence of their project or the funding could be cut tomorrow.

"Strictly speaking," he addressed himself not so much to Vlas as to Glavny, "most people do get something from our new technique, like increased relaxation, confidence, efficiency, etcetera. This could be a significant by-product of our research, since we do need a technique to combat the strains and tensions of modern life."

"Look," Glavny's eyes narrowed to a slit, "you aren't telling me that you've wasted all this time and millions of rubles in order to discover a nerve-soother — something that I could get from a sauna and a glass of beer? You know we want more than that. What about all that 'unspeakable bliss,' 'the Kingdom of Heaven,' which the priests used to talk about in their sermons? Was it just one of the tricks used by the clergy to delude the masses?"

Dr Larchuk looked hesitant about answering the question, but Dr Kon came quickly to his rescue.

"From what we could see during our experiment, it does appear, I am afraid, that these stories do have some basis in reality. The few individuals who responded to our technique most dramatically seemed to have undergone a profound experience, far more pleasant and uplifting than anything else they could recall. We cannot prove this conclusively, but we strongly suspect that most prominent religious mystics and saints did belong to the ST type, highly prone to this sort of experience. But, of course, their 'mystical' insights were later exploited and misrepresented by the clergy in order to distract the masses from their revolutionary struggle."

Vlas leaned towards Glavny and whispered in his ear, "Remember, I always told you there was a grain of truth in priests' and monks' tales and you used to pooh-pooh it. What do you say now?"

Glavny brushed this remark aside impatiently. "This is no time for jokes, Vlas. It's too serious."

"You two, tell me," he addressed himself directly to Drs Kon and Larchuk, "what are the practical results of your research? You are not advocating that we go back to Sunday schools and the Bible? Organize competitions for the largest percentage of burping meditators per factory? Give Orders of Lenin to the spiritual Stakhanovites who fall into your 0.05% ST category? I almost smell something vaguely subversive about all this," he concluded ominously.

Now it was Dr Larchuk's turn to be on the offensive. "Comrade First Secretary, when we first agreed to undertake this research, we were assured of complete freedom from interference. We were told that objective results were the most important thing, no matter what their ideological complications. And now you accuse us of subversion. We cannot work productively unless we can be sure that we are free to pursue the most promising hypotheses, whether they agree with our ideology or not."

Glavny, red-faced and still puffing with indignation, kept silent. This was an effective defence. So many times in the past the eager and ignorant Party hacks had interfered with research and stifled findings which could have been of great value to the country. He had made it a rule that in sensitive and urgent areas of military research, the ablest and most trusted scientists would have complete freedom. Well, almost complete freedom... But he never regretted this rule more than he did now. What Dr Kon said struck at the core of his own beliefs about the malevolence of religion, beliefs to which he adhered ever more vehemently in his later years.

Perhaps too vehemently, for his defensiveness and his impatience with Vlas betrayed his own growing insecurity. His mother was a peasant and an ardent Orthodox believer, and childhood lessons are not easily forgotten.

There was an uneasy silence around the table.

Dr Larchuk decided finally to break it. "We must point out that most of our experimental subjects were, naturally, atheists who found no difficulty whatever in interpreting their experience in nonreligious terms. Unfortunately, the results caught us a little by surprise, and some people did acquire a somewhat more pronounced religious or even 'mystical' orientation as a result of our experiment. In the future, we could provide them with an appealing and a sufficiently elaborate substitute for religious dogma. There is no reason why their experiences should not be couched in scientific terms more suitable to our society."

"Here we go," murmured Glavny to himself resignedly. "First we have the hashish smuggled into our camp under the guise of 'Socialin' and now the 'opium of the people' becomes the religion of the proletariat. What else have our brilliant scientists got up to?"

Dr Larchuk, who could not hear what Glavny had said, continued. "At the moment, we are working on a number of refinements, which promise to make our non-drug technique even more effective. What we lack, however, is direct access to people who have a broad knowledge of the kind of experience we are trying to produce. We complained of this difficulty before, but were told that most such people were eliminated over the years from our society, in one way or another. The Russian Orthodox Church refused to provide any assistance, either. They seemed to regard the idea that ordinary people could have experiences comparable to those of the saints of the past as a sort of heresy. So we need assistance in this direction. It could make or break our whole project."

Vlas whispered something into Glavny's ear.

"Check once more and see if there is any fresh news," Glavny responded.

Vlas went to the telephone in a small recess at the back of the conference room, where his voice could not be heard. He came back in a few minutes, smiling broadly, and whispered something into Glavny's ear. Glavny raised his eyebrows but looked pleased.

"Vlas," he said, "I want the title of the Hero of the Soviet Union for the leader of the team who successfully completed the Bermuda Triangle operation; and an Order of the Red Flag to every team member. They have done a valuable job."

Other participants were looking at Glavny expectantly.

"Comrades," Glavny decided to break the news publicly, "you will get the man you need. If our scientists would work with the efficiency and zeal displayed by our Special Forces Unit," he added pointedly, "then this project could be assured of an early and successful completion.

"But," he continued, "do not hesitate to ask us for help in the future — we will do all we can to help you. And now," he pinned each participant with a penetrating gaze from under his bushy eyebrows, "we want results, practical results, not the Biblical mumbo-jumbo."

He emphasized the word "practical" with a karate-like chop.

"I hope that at the next meeting, which shall take place in a month's time, we will hear your results. And now to work, comrades."

He motioned Vlas to stay behind as the other participants respectfully shuffled out of the room.

The Yogi And The Inquisitor

"Switch on the toposcope," Dr Kon told her assistant. The screen lit up, showing a brilliant display of dazzling dots and rainbow-striped fluctuating lines, running from one end of the screen to another, like waves in a pond.

"A most unusual pattern!" gushed the assistant. Dr Kon did not respond, engrossed in her observation of the screen.

"Turn it off," she called finally. "And please bring me computer analysis of the EEG." The assistant tore four or five feet of printout from the printer and put it on the table in front of Dr Kon. She studied the rows of figures attentively, murmuring to herself, "Very, very interesting..."

The door of the lab flew open and the silence was shattered by a loud voice, which Dr Kon immediately recognized as Vlas's.

"We have to secure his complete cooperation if we are to produce the results as quickly as Glavny wants them," Vlas was saying.

Dr Larchuk, who was walking behind him, was responding weakly, "Yes, I agree, Comrade Bur, but I think we should proceed with extreme caution. You must realize that voluntary cooperation would be by far the best for our purposes..."

Without lifting her head from the printout, Dr Kon called out excitedly to Dr Larchuk. "Look at these infraslow oscillations. I've never imagined that they could be of such magnitude. It is obvious that the pleasure circuitry is completely integrated with the hippocampal circuit, the proprioperceptive, and the sensory areas in the cortex."

"And what does the computer say?" Dr Larchuk seemed excited.

Dr Kon pointed to the printout. "You can see that our guess was correct. He definitely has the ST type brain

48

circuitry. But the degree of integration of the pleasure response is nothing short of astonishing. Certainly, we've never seen anything like this in our experimental subjects before."

Vlas was also looking at the computer printout as if trying to decipher something. "So you mean he belongs to your 0.05%, become-a-saint-in-ten-easy-steps category?" he quipped.

"Yes, he does, but he also has come a long way since he had the first experience," Dr Kon answered.

"Now, what I'd like to find out is how he's managed to achieve such complete neural and somatic integration," Dr Larchuk said thoughtfully. "It seems that he is experiencing uninterrupted pleasure alongside with all his internal and external perceptions and even thought processes. He is in a state of perpetual bliss, yet he appears to function completely normally."

"And look at the physiological measurements," Dr Kon pointed to another graph. Pulse rate is 35 per minute, breathing — 6 per minute, electrical skin conductance shows very little fluctuation from a low base reading, blood lactate and cortisol are extremely low. Everything is pointing to a degree of relaxation that we usually find only in deep sleep. Yet the man is obviously very much awake. He was looking through a Russian magazine when we took the measurements," marveled Dr Kon.

"Now tell me," Vlas adopted the slightly offended tone of a person who objected to being left out of the conversation because of his lack of knowledge, "what does all this nonsense mean? I remember reading an article about our champion runner Vladimir Kuts who, in his heyday as a runner had a resting pulse of 35 beats per minute. Does this mean that this Indian monk can run as fast as our Kuts?"

Dr Larchuk looked at Vlas with an air of consternation. "Comrade Bur, what was the greatest pleasure you've ever felt?"

Vlas thought for a second. "Well, like any normal man, I enjoy a drink, especially after a hot sauna, and in good company," he thundered with his cough-like laughter, "of pretty women."

"Now," continued Dr Larchuk, "imagine that all these pleasures could be combined into one, multiplied a thousand times, and that you could feel it no matter what you were doing. This is how this man feels, if we are to believe the EEG readings."

"I, for one, do not believe it," retorted Vlas. "I'd die of pleasure — or boredom — if I had to feel it all the time."

"Dr Larchuk oversimplified the picture somewhat," intervened Dr Kon. "Because the pleasure perceived is so strong and so constant, it is not felt in the ordinary way in which the pleasures you mentioned are. True, neither the body nor the mind could endure such constant state of rapture. So the body has to adapt, to become so extremely tranquil. It is like having the pleasure of sex with a pretty woman while listening to a beautiful piece of classical music instead of rowdy dancing."

"This is exactly what I mean," Vlas gleefully jumped at the analogy. "I am totally bored with classical music. I'll have rowdy dancing anytime."

"But if you learned to appreciate classical music, you would no longer be bored with it, or even want to go back to rowdy dancing," pointed out Dr Larchuk.

"But I *never* will like classical music, OK?" Vlas was becoming slightly irate.

"OK! OK!" Dr Kon backed down. "I used classical music just as an example. I mean something, whatever it is, that will give you the combined pleasure of wine, women, and song, many times over. Wouldn't you like to know what it is like?"

"No, I would not... because ... because ... it is unnatural. Man's got to have his fun the way he was made to feel it, and not in some weird, artificial way."

"Made by whom?" Dr Larchuk felt he was cornering his opponent.

"Look, you can't catch me," Vlas laughed derisively. "I can say anything I want. I can say God, or natural selection, or our Party made man that way. But we've got to do things the way they were intended."

"Even if it leads to the kind of social disruption that Glavny spoke about?" Dr Larchuk produced his last trump card. Vlas almost said, "Yes," in the heat of argument, but then changed his mind.

It was not wise even for him to contradict Glavny in other people's company. From the very beginning, he had felt rather dubious about this whole project. It struck him as being sort of... batty. Now his vague suspicions were becoming confirmed.

He had only agreed to accept the responsibility for the Project because the rewards as promised by Glavny were too great to refuse, and the punishment for not accepting the honor even greater. He was now sure that the whole thing, cooked up by these smart-alecky eggheads from the Institute was going to come to naught, like so many of their hare-brained schemes in the past. A new project, lots of money squandered, medals all round, and then — a bust, denunciations, demotions, and even, in more dramatic cases, arrests and executions. Oh, no. He was going to make sure that at least he didn't get his head chopped off when the day of reckoning came.

But for a while yet, it was better to go along with the tide, collecting as many alibis for himself as possible along the way. Later, he could always find some fall guys, like he did in the past.

"I wonder if we'll be able to find out how he has managed to combine such cortical-subcortical integration with such low arousal," Dr Larchuk was musing aloud. "I wonder if he will — or even can — convey it."

"Ask him," Vlas was eager to make some sort of contribution to the discussion. "Why do you think we went to such lengths? To procure him sitting there looking so pretty with that spaceman helmet on his head?"

He pointed towards the one-way mirror glass, which separated the lab from the subject's cubicle. In it, under a large helmet used for measuring brain waves from the deepest areas of the brain, was the white-clad figure of Swami. He presented a rather unusual sight, with wires and tubes entangling his frail body, but somehow he still managed to retain an air of dignity.

"Ask him," Vlas insisted. "And if he refuses to cooperate, tell him that we can run the current through that helmet in the reverse direction," he guffawed again. "He'll tell us everything he knows then."

Dr Kon was appalled. "Comrade Vlas, I beg you not to talk like that. We run a scientific laboratory, not a torture chamber... This man is... I suppose in the old times you used to call them saints or holy men. But whatever he is, he will not respond to the kind of rough treatment you are advocating. Don't you remember from history how people like him went joyously to the gallows and to the stake without compromising their beliefs? I insist that his cooperation be absolutely voluntary."

Yes, deep down, Vlas knew this. He was not too familiar with ancient history, but he knew from personal experience that Dr Kon was speaking the truth. What didn't they do to those little saints in the thirties! The Spanish Inquisitors were inept amateurs compared to the NKVD interrogators like Vlas. And yet, despite the abominable humiliations, pain, and deprivation, many of these fanatics clung to their beliefs. Vlas could not understand what made them impervious to the pressures that unfailingly broke down even the strongest of Communists, and, because of this personal feeling of impotence and disbelief; he hated them and tortured them all the more.

But he knew that this time he had to keep his feelings under control.

They went into a small conference room. In a few minutes, the assistant brought in Swami. Dr Larchuk, being the only one who spoke good English, introduced Vlas to him as "a senior government official, interested in the application of psychological techniques to social problems."

"What is the nature of the problem?" enquired Swami in a lively voice.

"Well, I guess," Dr Larchuk hesitated for a second, "we want to make our people more happy and productive and less willing to indulge in destructive social and recreational activities, like drugs and alcohol."

"This appears to be a noble goal. And do the leaders also want to become more enlightened?"

Dr Larchuk translated the question to Vlas.

"Tell him that we have not thought it out that far yet," answered Vlas diplomatically. "Our present goal is to increase the contentment and the productivity of the masses. Ask him if he is willing to help us."

Swami listened attentively to the translation but did not hurry with his reply. "Is this the request of the top leaders of the country?" he asked finally.

"Yes, the very top," replied Vlas through his interpreter. Swami thought again for a long time. Vlas impatiently beat out a rhythm with his fingernails.

"OK," Swami declared finally, "I will help you. But tell me first what exactly you want to know."

Vlas sighed with relief while Dr Kon looked at her pad of prepared questions.

"First of all, we want to know if the technique you are advocating is universally effective."

"Yes, it is universally effective," answered Swami confidently.

"But in our experiments we find that only a small proportion of people respond dramatically, or have what we call a 'pronounced pleasure response'," objected Dr Larchuk.

"Are you sure you are using the right meditation?" asked Swami.

"Yes, in fact, we incorporated about 90% of the technique you use into our own version."

"How did you find out about the mantras and the way to choose them?"

"Well," Dr Larchuk sounded slightly embarrassed, "we have our own ways of finding these things out."

"Oh," Swami gave an understanding nod, "you got some of my teachers to co-operate with you. But you find it still does not work well enough for everybody?"

"It did produce some relaxation and a release of tension, but very few people felt any degree of intense pleasure. And this is what we want."

"Every step in this meditation, even if it manifests itself only as a mild relaxation, is a tiny step towards ultimate bliss, which the individual would never have taken otherwise," answered Swami proudly.

"How long would it take for an average person to obtain this 'ultimate bliss'?" Vlas was eager to find out.

"It will depend on the amount of stress accumulated by the nervous system. It could be 5, 10, 13, 20, or 50 years. For some, it may be many lifetimes. What is important to remember, though, is that from the very first day, happiness, both in the individual and in the society around him, will, however imperceptibly, grow. Without the meditation, suffering and pain would have continued to grow. So, instead of winning a million dollars, you would have lost a million — and ended up two million dollars poorer." Swami laughed, obviously delighted with his analogy.

"Five to fifty years?" Vlas exclaimed, "But we cannot wait that long! We want results now, and on a large scale. Can we make it work faster?"

"You could make it act a bit faster if your government gave my technique its full support, like setting up large meditation centers and weekend retreats where people could meditate more intensively. But you cannot force evolution. If you go too fast, you get into a blind alley and will have to retrace your steps," said Swami adamantly.

Vlas could not argue with this sentiment. He remembered how once they had tried to force evolution by breeding "miracle" hybrid vegetables, which supposedly defied the laws of agriculture and selection to produce greater yields. The results were disastrous. Once again, he felt that their "Project Nirvana" was doomed to failure. He looked at his watch and announced that he had to go as he had an urgent appointment in the Kremlin.

As he was leaving the room, Vlas heard Dr Kon say, "Do you think you could answer a few technical questions about your meditation, and especially the advanced techniques? It would be of great assistance to us."

"Ask your questions," replied Swami.

"At least I could report to Glavny that he is cooperating," thought Vlas. "We will save the bad news for the future when I find someone to blame."

A black limousine was waiting for him at the entrance. "Kremlin!" he called out to the driver, taking a packet of Camels out of his pocket. "And fast."

The car drove out of the narrow street in which the Institute was located and, reaching the wide Avenue of Peace, accelerated to 80 miles an hour. The traffic officers, recognizing the familiar limousine with its MOC number plates, stopped the traffic to give it a green light. As it sped past, other drivers and pedestrians gave it the look of mixed curiosity combined with vague envy and resentment.

Dr Larchuk's Discovery

Dr Larchuk left the Institute late that night. He decided not to drive home in his new Moskvich that he was recently given for his project. He just could not face the anxious questions that his gloomy and tired face would inevitably provoke from his wife. Ever since she had learned he was doing top-secret work for the government, she had become unbearably over-solicitous, scanning his expression for the slightest hint of worry. She presumed, perhaps not incorrectly, that his future career, and maybe even freedom, was dependent on the success or failure of this secret work.

"That trickster, that schemer, that two-faced bastard!" Dr Larchuk almost convulsed with indignation at the very thought of Vlas. He had just come out of the late meeting with Vlas and Dr Kon. They had been told that Glavny was unhappy about the progress of their research. Only a few days were left until the fateful monthly review meeting with Glavny. The nearer the day of reckoning approached, the more depressed he and Dr Kon became.

Not that they had not done a great deal during the past three weeks. Much had been accomplished; some new and exciting avenues for research had been opened. But results, ready, usable, *practical* results of the kind that Vlas and Glavny wanted — they were still beyond their reach.

And now Vlas was trying to shift the blame onto them. He accused them of pussyfooting in their research, of mollycoddling the Indian guru instead of demanding or even extracting information from him, of not starting a new series of experiments soon enough on the basis of the data already collected. He could not understand — or refused to, for reasons best known to himself — that the psychological states they were dealing with were extremely subtle, almost completely unknown to science, and potentially dangerous when applied to normal people on a mass scale.

It was of course possible that Swami was withholding

some information from them, answering their questions evasively. But they had no way of combating this. For one thing, if they put pressure on him, what guarantee did they have that he would not provide them with some misleading information? None. With his superior knowledge of the subject, he could play as many tricks on them as he liked.

Dr Larchuk stumbled and almost fell over a grey, shapeless mass lying in front of him on the sidewalk. The mass groaned and cursed at him.

"A drunk, another blessed drunk," he thought with disgust.

He was walking along a badly-lit portion of the Rostokinski Avenue, bordering on the Sokolniki Park. He had scarcely gone another fifty meters before he saw another drunk, doubled up, retching among the trees.

Dr Larchuk knew that it was the end of the month and a payday. He almost regretted not having taken the car home. All he needed to complete his misfortune was to be assaulted by one of these wretches.

He decided to hail a taxi. There were plenty of them passing by, but none of them heeded his frantic waving. It was considered a bad spot, especially on a Friday night. Finally, a taxi stopped and the driver, after suspiciously eyeing him for signs of inebriation, unlocked the rear door.

"Where to?" he asked brusquely.

Dr Larchuk thought for a moment. No, he was still not ready to go home. He needed time to mull a few things over, to relax a bit after the hard day. He told the driver to go to a restaurant off Gorki Street that he used to occasionally stop by in his days as a bachelor.

The restaurant was packed, but he was able to secure himself a table after waiting for half an hour in vain and then surreptitiously slipping a ten-ruble note into the hand of the doorkeeper, a sum he would have ordinarily considered excessive.

He ordered a bottle of red wine and a kebab.

He was led to a corner table with just one other person occupying it. They introduced themselves. His companion for the evening was an engineer from a small provincial town in Central Russia. He was dressed in an expensive but poorly tailored ready-made striped suit and was ill at ease in the plush surroundings of a Moscow restaurant.

"You like Moscow?" Dr Larchuk asked in a friendly tone, trying to make his neighbour feel more at home.

The engineer smiled back with effusiveness of a provincial.

"Yep, a great town. I still have to visit the Kremlin and the Lenin's tomb, but I have already made my trip well worth the bother," he announced proudly, "I bought two cases of imported cognac from a clever Georgian fellow that I met by chance, you know, selling the kind of brandy you never see in our area, and a pair of shoes for my wife, Polish-made — and for myself, a nice winter coat, the kind you can only get on the black market back home at three times the price. I wish I'd lived closer to Moscow."

The band returned to the stage after a break. To Dr Larchuk's dismay, it was not the traditional band that had played light music when he was in the restaurant a few years back. Even that band, relatively tame, disagreed with his musical tastes, but he had become used to the melodies and had learned to disregard them as a sort of "white noise." Not this collection of musical savages. The long-haired and jeans-attired "musicians" were armed with electric guitars, a saxophone, an electric piano, and a huge array of drums and other noise-producing implements. They were doing the Russian version of a popular song by Tom Jones who was then becoming something of an idol to the Russian pop fans.

The diners went wild at the "Oh, Delilah" refrain. Dr Larchuk's companion, though slightly overwhelmed by the loud and unfamiliar sounds, was stamping his feet in tune with the music. His bottle of cheap brandy was half-empty already, and he was getting increasingly tipsy.

No, it did not look like Dr Larchuk was going to have much of a chance to reflect peacefully over a glass of wine. He looked around the restaurant. Sweaty, animated faces, with half-opened mouths and wide-open, though, to him, vacant eyes, demanding more excitement, louder music, more cheap cognac. More and more — despite the splitting hangovers the next day, the absenteeism, the battered wives and children, despite the present and future ulcers and nervous breakdowns, they all just wanted to have "good time."

Dr Larchuk felt as if this whole throbbing mass of bodies and sounds enveloping him was a physical force, like a hurricane, pounding against him. Would he — or even Glavny — be able to stem this tsunami of human longing before it engulfed them and their god-forsaken country, nay, the whole world? The world that will be converted into a junk-yard of electrified, plastic mass culture? Could they hope to counteract the inevitable side effects of the all-engulfing consumer society, with its alcohol and drug addiction, crime, and alienation?

He felt hopeless. He was faced by an evolutionary force, not just a soulless tsunami, but a herd of wild bison, ready to break through the puny barriers erected by social tradition and Communist propaganda. Evolution was on the side of the naked ape, whose fervent search for gratification demanded and then swallowed everything that science and technology and the Earth's still bountiful resources could provide.

"If only man could evolve faster," he thought wistfully, as the sounds of the song died down amid the undulating shrills of the electric guitar and the crescendo of the drums, with the crowd jumping to their feet and throwing five-ruble notes on the stage.

If only man could find pleasure in the more refined, less disruptive pursuits... If only he could learn to be stimulated by the allure of knowledge that was the driving force for people like him.

And yet, and yet... Who provided these masses with the

power to make their electric didgeridoos sound so thunderously? Who developed the entire scientific structure that gave life these ugly shapes and sounds? It was people like him, pursuing their "sublime" scientific gratifications.

One Einstein, misused and misdirected, can cause more damage to the Earth and to humanity than millions of these wild revellers.

He knew very well that the fruits of his research would fall into the unscrupulous hands of the Glavnys and the Vlases of this world. Glavny came as close as anyone to be the embodiment of a brute, a Neanderthal armed with a nuclear bomb.

Did he, Larchuk, know what potential harm was going to result from his research in ten, or twenty, or fifty years time?

He had to admit that he had no idea. His idealistic strivings had not changed much since his student days when he wrote a paper on using recombinant DNA techniques to make humans photosynthesise their food, like plants — the only way, he felt, mankind could be purged of its predatory and destructive evolutionary legacy.

As Dr Larchuk gazed around the restaurant again, his feeling of superiority vanished. He was also part of the mob. He was just as hooked as they were. He only judged his type of satisfaction superior to their kind because that was what he was conditioned to crave.

The dichotomy of classical music and rowdy dancing, which he and Dr Kon had given to Vlas was all wrong. His preference for the former was a class and education-based value, a cultural preference, nothing more than that.

"To transcend human nature," he wrote feverishly on his napkin, struck by a sudden realization, "one first has to realize the common roots of the animalistic and the sublime, and then transcend them both."

For him, drugs, immoderate drinking, and indulgent sex were animalistic; classical music, intellectual search, and meditation were sublime. But both somehow tapped the same source of satisfaction in the human brain. If only one could somehow harmonize and then redirect these two drives of human nature... for peace... for healing the wounded planet from human greed, overpopulation, and pollution...

Dr Larchuk was doodling with his finger in a little pool of liquid spilt from his wine glass. He was now oblivious to his neighbor and to the blaring music of the new song that filled the room.

"To harmonize and to transcend ... the animalistic and the sublime..."

Something exploded in his gut — he was sure it was not in his brain — that filled him with the radiant glow of the eureka moment.

"Supersoma XL-14!"

The gentle, side effect-free Supersoma! But — combined with meditation! This was the magic brew that would open the gates of Paradise! For everyone! The drug — which was plant-derived — and the meditation were working in the same direction, but taken separately, neither was powerful enough. It was his rejection of his competitors' research, his habitual disdain for drugs, all drugs, that had prompted this oversight. No doubt Dr Abosov's team thought that his research was also nebulous and impractical. They were both bloody stubborn fools...

Now, he had something to report to Vlas and Glavny.

He jumped from his table and ran to the cloakroom, clutching the tag he was given in exchange for his coat. The waiter ran after him in hot pursuit, demanding payment. He put his hand into his wallet and, without looking, shoved some banknotes into the waiter's hand. As he went through the door, he heard the stunned voice of the waiter, "Thank you, comrade, thank you... Sir... thank you for your generosity."

Richard Snowden's Rebirth

Snowden was lying in his bed, staring at the ceiling. It was the third day he had spent in this passive, withdrawn mood. They came in to give him some food; he ate it, went to the toilet, and returned to bed to look at the ceiling with the same vacant stare. A doctor came in, measured his temperature, blood pressure, looked at his eyes and tongue, and left, shrugging his shoulders.

In the last few days, Snowden's vision of himself had shrunk from that of a global military strategist to that of an occupant of a small prison-like cell. And now it had shrunk even further — to a dimly-lit point somewhere inside his skull, which kept continually posing him some huge and ultimately unanswerable question.

His debriefing was finished. At first, he felt bad about giving them any information at all. As he saw that they would not give up and might even torture him, he began to tell them a little about his work, but continued to withhold any sensitive data. However, he had to grant that the KGB or the GRU — or whoever was questioning him — knew what they were doing and expected him to behave exactly as he did. The whole team set upon him methodically, backed up by an unknown number of experts who checked and cross-checked everything he said. Every lead he gave was relentlessly followed up, and whenever he left some gaps or they found inconsistencies, they demanded clarification. They pressured him by increasing or decreasing the small liberties which, to a man imprisoned, can make the difference between bearable purgatory and sheer hell.

But in the end it was neither the constant pressure nor their interrogating skills that made him gradually start to crack up. To his own surprise, he began to reveal certain ideas of his own free will, even things that they did not really ask him for.

As he listened to their questions anticipating their guesses and speculations, he realized that for the past fifteen years, he had lived a life in a universe parallel to that of his interrogators. In the minds of the Soviet military experts who came to debrief him, Richard could see the same suspicion and paranoia, the mirror image of his own and fellow workers' worldview. The Soviets, he discovered, were animated by the same ideas as the Americans, only in reverse. They also looked at their American counterparts as treacherous and potentially violent barbarians who needed somehow to be contained, lest the world fall prey to their cunning and greed. It was suspicion breeding suspicion. As soon as one side postulated that the other side was gaining a new edge on weaponry (often incorrectly), it would search for an answer to this new challenge. This, in turn, would confirm the worst suspicions of the other side. Thus, the growing spiral of weaponry pressed onward. Attempts to curb it were timid and ineffectual and were due not so much to the renunciation of suspicion as to the unbearable costs and potential dangers of new weapons to anyone, including the victors in any war.

If there was any intelligence or rationality in this whole macabre and infinitely escalating scenario, it certainly did not seem to reside in the minds of those who pushed it along. All that seemed to improve and become more sophisticated were the weapon systems themselves, which their human inventors served. Of course, there were sophisticated equations that underpinned the Mutually Assured Destructions (MAD) scenarios that they have worked on. Richard personally knew one of the experts who would later be given a Nobel Prize in science (and yet later diagnosed with paranoid schizophrenia). There were civilian offshoots of their work, where civil administrators of huge systems, like the health system in Britain, attempted to copy some of their formulas and apply them to people in order to increase their productivity. Richard, without knowing what the Soviets were aiming for, could feel that they pursued similar goals: not only to prove that their system was superior to any one else's (the ultimate proof being a win in any future war, including nuclear war), but that they also possessed the key to making people behave like obedient, and productive, machines not just on the battlefield but also in their ordinary lives.

He started having nightmares and was wondering if the Soviets were not slipping something in his food or drinks to unbalance him. One night, he could swear that he was awake and that he saw his dead girlfriend, dressed in a white shroud, appear at the foot of his bed, staring at him accusingly. He woke up, or came to, trembling violently.

Strange thoughts began to appear in his mind. Could it be that the development of ever more sophisticated weaponry had a rationale of its own, as yet impenetrable to the human mind? If so, what was that rationale? To what twisted part of the human mind/brain system was it hinged? Could it even be connected to some source of unknown, outside malevolent intelligence?

Worn out by endless questioning and sleepless nights, Richard was becoming more and more focused on such problems, until something in his mind finally snapped. It did not seem to matter anymore whether he gave the information they requested to him or withheld it. What was the use of hiding a trump card in his sleeve when the rules of the game were not known even to the players? And if they were known to somebody — or something — outside of them, then surely that higher arbiter knew every card in the pack, and also who, if anyone, would win in the end.

Did life really have a meaning? Or was his consciousness nothing more than the puppet upon which Nature — or God — played out this illogical spectacle? Richard was no longer even thinking of his cozy unit overlooking the lake in Croton-on-Hudson, nor his German Shepherd, Rekki, which used to give him comfort in the past. Mrs Greemshaw, his neighbor, would surely take good care of the abandoned canine. Working in the secret government business for many years, divorced, and remaining single for the past few years had taught him to keep to himself. He would not be missed much at work or at home. Yes, the dog might miss him for a while but then get used to his new owners.

There was a knock at the door. Richard rolled over to face the wall. He did not want to talk to the officer who regularly brought in his meals. He found the officer's attempts to cheer him up with a few badly translated Russian jokes pathetic. Now that they had squeezed him dry of everything he knew, he was no use to anyone. He had become a non-person. He only wished they would leave him alone.

The door opened and into the room marched Vlas accompanied by Dr Larchuk.

That evening, Richard was transferred to the Institute. Dr Larchuk was eager to verify his hypothesis that the combination of meditation and the drug based on genetically modified psychedelic Siberian mushroom would work. He was eager to carry out some preliminary tests the very next morning, using Richard as a guinea pig. He explained to Snowden that they were testing a new psychotherapeutic technique, which could help relieve his depression. "What depression?" Richard thought apprehensively. Were they going to treat his existential quest as depression?

He became a little more interested in what they were proposing when they told him that the method was derived from an ancient Vedic tradition, and that Swami was involved in the project. Recently, Richard was actually going over in his mind some of the things that he had discussed with Swami in the submarine during their chess games and finding that Swami's ideas were not as crazy as some theories at Hudson.

He was sitting under the EEG helmet, staring blankly into space. In the laboratory, Dr Larchuk was speaking to Dr Kon. "He is ideal for our purposes. Very little cross-talk between the limbic area and the frontal lobes. He is a pure Apollonian, a very rational person who is largely ruled by his intellect. His emotions are well under control on the surface, although, of course, deep down, he is also ruled by them like all humans.

"Ordinarily, he would have no chance at all of homing into the pleasure areas by means of some traditional meditation technique. It would take him months, possibly years, before he could even attain deep relaxation. He is too much "in this head," caught up in his thoughts and ideas. Right now, he seems on the verge of a neurotic, or maybe a psychotic, breakdown."

Dr Larchuk went over to the experimental cubicle. "Mr. Snowden," he said, "I want you to take this little pill now. It will intensify the effects of the meditation technique that I will instruct you in. Don't worry; the pill is absolutely harmless, made from a plant-derived material. The active substance had been used by natives in Siberia for centuries, without any ill effects. In fact, it made them stronger physically and psychologically. It is very quick-acting and will also completely get out of your system in the next couple of hours.

"Now, this is the sound I want you to repeat in your mind effortlessly during meditation."

He whispered a short, meaningless syllable into Richard's ear. "Begin to say it with me... that's right... and now with your eyes closed... more quickly, and softly, and still more quickly and softly, and now just say it easily in your mind. If you find yourself distracted by something, just revert back to the sound I gave you. Keep doing this for a few minutes until I come back."

Dr Larchuk tiptoed out of the cubicle. "What's happening? Anything significant?" he asked Dr Kon, who was monitoring the toposcope screen.

Blue, red, and yellow dots were dancing across the screen, coming together and dispersing again like small flocks of sparrows scattering at someone's approach and then regrouping again. Now and again, the seemingly chaotic dance of the colored dots and strips would become synchronized, as though some unseen conductor was imposing order upon the confused sound of an orchestra tuning their instruments. These bursts of synchronized brain function were becoming more and more prolonged until, after a few minutes, the entire brain was responding to the directions of the invisible conductor, blending itself into one grand, harmonious tutti.

They could hardly believe their own eyes. They saw nothing like this when they were experimenting with the drug and meditation before. There were some episodes of partial harmony between the different areas of the brain but nothing like what was happening on the screen now.

They also knew that Dr Abosov's team was getting the same partial, insignificant result with meditation used alone.

Dr Larchuk was whispering, "The magic brew has opened the gate to paradise... this is the answer. For thousands of years man has searched in vain, through prayer and meditation, fasting and bodily modification... how simple, how sublime..."

Dr Kon turned away from the screen. There were tears in her eyes. She too understood the meaning of what they were witnessing. She too was experiencing the supreme satisfaction of finding the shining fragments of the philosopher's stone under the rubble of discarded and half-baked hypotheses. They embraced, forgetting for a moment their habitual reserve.

"Now that's very nice, I must say," a gruff voice spoke, "combining business and pleasure." Vlas had just entered the Laboratory. "Please continue, don't mind me, I am only a fly on the wall..."

Snowden was oblivious to all this. Blue, red, and yellow circles were appearing in his brain in rapid succession. Each repetition of the mantra was bringing in a new wave of color, which also seemed to resound in his ears, like a magic, mysterious sound.

"That's strange," Richard thought, "I never knew that one could *hear* colors." Ordinarily, he could not even see colors vividly. All his dreams were in black-and-white. Only once had he seen a dream in color, and even that was of a two-colored globe, with blue oceans and green forests.

"The Peace that passeth all understanding," he remembered the words he had read somewhere and thought how apt they were. The cares and burdens that had been crushing him just a few minutes before were melting away. He felt as though someone was washing and purifying him from within with a soft, caressing sponge.

"How silly it was of me to get all vexed about the world's problems," he thought. "This tranquility, this bliss... Life is joy."

Was this the meaning of life for which he had been vaguely searching all his life, but so desperately during these last few days? Could it be true? All those years wasted in useless, self-gratifying pursuits, futile relationships, striving for success, material comforts, and fame. He could have cried over the lost opportunities, the missed moments of happiness, of love and intimacy, but his eyes refused to shed tears.

Memories from his childhood began to float into his consciousness, without disturbing the calm sea of his awareness or interrupting the gentle, and now spontaneous, pulsation of his mantra. Snippets of dreams and nightmares were rising from the depths of his subconscious, disjointed and now somehow powerless. Images that ordinarily would have woken him shivering in cold sweat were now dissolving painlessly, neutralized by the healing presence he felt within.

Richard had a sensation as if his chest was expanding endlessly in one all-embracing inhalation, which made him feel huge, as big as the universe itself. He knew that this was an illusion and that his breathing was still, almost absent. Everything he experienced now was a paradox, a blending of impossibilities. Even the bright point of light with which he normally identified his consciousness was spilling beyond the barriers of his skull, filling the whole world with a radiant and uniform glow.

He could not think at that moment, and only had a sensation of rising — or falling — precipitously. He did not know how long this ascent – or descent — lasted. When he could think again, words formed in his mind, "Life is joy, and peace, and light... And I am that, too..."

Richard did not know how long he spent in this state. For some time, his mind was still anchored effortlessly in that pleasant and brightly lit world of oneness. Then he would be distracted momentarily by some noise or feeling. He could, for a time, immediately return to that sublime world by simply bringing back his mantra. But the breaks of normal consciousness were becoming longer and longer.

Dr Larchuk, who was observing his progress on the toposcope, came into the cubicle and whispered softly, "Just sit quietly for a few minutes, with your eyes closed and don't bring your mantra back consciously."

Finally, Richard opened his eyes. The world seemed to have gained some new, translucent quality. His mind and his body were light and pliable, as if he had shed some terrific burden.

"Doctor," he said, "I feel new, reborn. I feel... happy.

"You know something," he said, feeling mildly embarrassed, "Life is joy."

He smiled, looking Dr Larchuk straight in the eyes.

"Yes," Dr Larchuk averted his gaze. "Yes, I know how you must feel. I feel happy for you.

"Now, if you don't mind, a colleague of mine will ask you a few questions about your experience."

Vlas was waiting impatiently at the entrance to the cubicle.

Meditation Practiced Twice a Day...

The train was pulling out of the Taiga Station, heading north towards the city of Tomsk. The banners and posters decorating the near-derelict building of the station were speeding past the train windows, blending into a single incomprehensible blur: "Glory to... tons of pig iron... meditation... road to Communism."

A middle-aged peasant woman, loaded with baskets and net bags, was walking along the corridor looking for a vacant seat. Finally, she saw a compartment with only three people. Mumbling something under her breath, she heaved her load onto the luggage rack and sat down.

Soon, with the lack of inhibition that some outgoing peasant women possess, she told everyone in the compartment her story. She had recently slaughtered a pig, which she had fattened herself on her small lot in the village. The money would have been enough to buy not only new timber to repair the roof, but also to send a few things to her son who was studying agriculture in the city. But, she smiled apologetically; her old man soon took care of any extra money.

"He drinks, you know." So she salvaged what she could and was now going to take her son some salted pork and some jam she had made from wild berries picked in autumn.

He was doing very well in his studies, and he would become a farmer one day, but he needed solid, nourishing food to keep him healthy and clear-headed. She had been told that the food in the college canteen was awful.

A woman in her early thirties, fashionably dressed for these parts, was listening to her story sympathetically, adding a comment of her own now and again. A man in the corner, about forty years of age, in a conservatively cut suit with broad lapels, was reading a newspaper, pointedly ignoring the chatting women. A young girl, probably a student, was looking vacantly out of the window, where pine trees and snow-covered fields sped past the train in a monotonous filmstrip.

"Ah, so you're from Moscow," the old woman exclaimed, addressing herself to the fashionably dressed woman. "That's interesting. You know how cut off we are here. Tell me some of the latest news. What's new in the shops? Is it really true that they've erected some funny-looking statue over Nikita Khrushchev's grave? And what's this new thing about... what do you call it? Meditation?"

The young woman explained patiently, "Yes, that's true about Khrushchev, but it's not a big statue, it's a head, actually, framed by black and white stones. I've seen it myself...

"The latest fashion in Moscow are leather boots from Czechoslovakia, reaching up to mid-thigh, fifty rubles a pair. However," here the Muscovite lowered her voice confidentially, "rumor has it that volume of sales in Moscow shops have fallen drastically, and some people attribute it to the introduction of meditation. People just aren't so crazy about acquiring possessions anymore."

"Tell me what this meditation business is all about," the countrywoman inquired.

"Well, it's a form of mental gymnastics our scientists have recently discovered. It makes people more efficient, happier. They say that productivity in factories where workers use Socialin together with meditation has doubled."

"What's Socialin?"

"Oh, it's a little red pill you take before you do your meditation, something like a vitamin pill. They say it makes you feel good. Apparently, lots of people stopped drinking vodka as soon as they began taking Socialin."

"That would sure be a God-sent pill for my old man," sighed the woman. "I wonder when we will get it in our village... We always get everything last, whether it's imported boots or this... Socialin thing.

"Now tell me, have you taken it yourself? Is it, like... compulsory?" The old woman was curious to know, mostly for the sake of her husband.

"No, I haven't taken it myself because I wasn't working at the time, and in the beginning they were only issuing Socialin through your workplace. But it's completely voluntary. However, most people who took it want to take it again, and they tell their friends about it. So it's spreading like wildfire. Some people were even getting smart and storing the pills away to sell them on the black market. But the authorities soon put a stop to that. Now they will only issue the pill if you come to the meditation center, and you have to take it there and then, and do your meditation," the woman explained patiently.

"But to answer your question about how it feels, well, people who have taken it say that it feels like heaven. It makes you forget all your worries and problems, and you feel so fresh afterwards. Some knowledgeable people even say privately that it makes you feel different about the world, like the way they say some religious types felt in the past."

"Now that's a blatant lie and a gross distortion!" The man in the corner could no longer contain himself. He pointed to the newspaper he was reading. "Don't you read the papers? Listen to what it says here, in this article." He began to read, carefully stressing each sentence.

"'Despite some rumors spread by malicious and ignorant people'," he pointedly looked up from the paper, "meditation has nothing to do with religion. The theoretical basis for this profoundly socialist practice was laid long ago by the classics of Marxism-Leninism.' See? And there are some quotations from the classics to prove the point."

The older woman was getting bored and tried to bring the conversation back to the imported boots. But the man could not be stopped.

"And, it says further, 'Our brilliant scientists have now come up with practical confirmation of the profound insights of our Marxist leaders, who felt that the advancement of our people towards the goal of Communism should take place on every front: material, scientific, moral, and now, psychological. We finally have a practical and dependable tool provided by our scientists to make that prediction come true.' So you see? No religious mumbo-jumbo, straight science, everything clear and predictable."

"And I've heard," the student girl volunteered rather shyly, "that it makes people feel younger."

"Well, there may well be some truth in that," confirmed the man with the newspaper authoritatively. "I read recently in the journal, *Knowledge is Strength*, that they are carrying out experiments to test the effects of meditation on longevity."

"Well, all I wish is that they'd send some of this stuff to our village, to stop my old man from drinking us into total poverty," said the old woman. "I would certainly thank the Party in my prayers, along with all those clever scientists."

The train pulled into the next station. Among the older and weather-beaten posters, there were freshly-printed ones, proclaiming:

Meditation
Practiced Twice a Day
Will Further the Cause of Communism
And Wash ALL Your Problems Away

Larchuk Defects

Dr Larchuk closed the door of his office, now adorned with a bronze plaque reading, "Government Honorary Scientific Adviser." He had been awarded this new title at the Academy of Sciences in recognition of his work of implementing Socialin in conjunction with meditation. He had been elevated to the very top of the scientific hierarchy and was given the appropriate privileges. A spacious office in the Academy's building, in addition to his old laboratory at the Institute, a new three-bedroom flat almost next door to Glavny's city apartment on Kutuzovsky Prospect; a luxurious, state-subsidized country house (the much coveted *dacha*) at Nikolina Gora, and access to the elite's closed shopping facility on Granovsky Street.

Today, for the first time since that fateful eureka moment at the restaurant, Dr Larchuk did not feel like going home. This was despite the fact that his wife was eagerly awaiting him to show off the new wallpaper from Finland she had finally managed to obtain using her connections. He had phoned her earlier to say that he will work late.

Dr Larchuk opened a small compartment on the side of his bookshelf and produced a bottle of green Chartreuse. He found that little sips of this liqueur, produced long ago by far-away French monks, were much more conducive to creative reverie than his previously-favored local port. Lately though he found himself indulging in his newly-found preference a little too frequently.

Not that things were not going smoothly for Dr Larchuk at work or at home. On the contrary he would not have been able to pinpoint a single problem in his new life that was worthy of attention. The few minor snags that had cropped up during the initial stages of the project had been ironed out. True, it had looked at one stage as though human nature was going to defeat their plans. As soon as it was discovered that Socialin — even without meditation — could provide one

75

with a free high, people began hoarding the pills and then selling them on the black market at a hefty price. Then a group of chemistry students in Nizhnyi Novgorod had cracked Socialin's complicated plant-derived formula and had started a small kitchen-sink factory to produce a revamped chemical version of the drug. They were all sentenced to twenty-five years of hard labor in Far Eastern camps. But Glavny and Vlas could never be sure whether that was sufficient to discourage other entrepreneurs from trying to cash in on the government's latest crazy scheme.

At one stage, the situation seemed to be getting so much out of hand that Glavny, despite the scientists' plea to wait and see, was on the verge of banning Socialin altogether and terminating the project. Party officials were contemplating the introduction of the death penalty for unauthorized possession of the drug.

However, after a while, as the scientists observed an advanced experimental group, they noticed a strange phenomenon. Gradually, people who took Socialin combined with meditation stopped craving the drug. Their overall level of contentment rose, and they were no longer prepared to go to any lengths to procure the drug. It was the strangest case of addiction they had ever seen — an addiction that cured itself. There were still a few people who took Socialin alone, without the meditation, but its effects were minimal compared to that produced in combination with meditation; so they too soon gave up. The black market profiteers and kitchen-sink chemists were going out of business.

Undoubtedly, Project Nirvana was a resounding success. The rate of alcoholism in Moscow, the first experimental city, dropped by seventy-five per cent in the first six months. Crime and juvenile delinquency rates declined significantly. Productivity in some enterprises jumped by 200 per cent. The government was considering doubling the GNP growth forecast for the current Five Year Plan.

Yet Dr Larchuk, now a Hero of Socialist Labor and holder of innumerable other official awards, was far from happy. In fact, he now often dreamed of his stressful but creative student days. They seemed now to have a romantic flavor, an excitement, a sense of true discovery. In comparison, his present life was becoming somehow dull and monotonous.

He wanted to pour himself another small glass of Chartreuse, but changed his mind. His gaze fell on a packet of Socialin lying on top of his desk. He turned away. No, that stuff wasn't for him. He had always hated drugs. But then... and he looked at the bottle of Chartreuse, wasn't that also a drug? For sure more harmful than Socialin. Impulsively, Dr Larchuk took out one pill and swallowed it. With a tremendous sigh of relief, he walked across his office to a comfortable armchair, sat down, and closed his eyes.

When Dr Larchuk left his office an hour or so later, he left a piece of paper pinned to his secretary's calendar. It read: "As of today I wish to resign all my posts and commissions with the government and would like to devote myself solely to research on the evolutionary function of the neomammalian and paleomammalian cortex, the research which has been interrupted by recent engagements. Dr Anastas Larchuk." Then he added, after some hesitation:

"P. S. Comrades, life is joy."

A few days later, the following confidential circular letter was released by the Central Committee:

"To all members of the central government, Heads of Party organizations, Senior scientific, military, and industrial personnel:

While the use of meditation alone has been found to be of value to top Party and government workers who are endowed with great responsibility and often working under considerable pressure, the combined use of meditation and Socialin is from now on strictly forbidden to all aforementioned personnel. Anyone using Socialin or found to be in unauthorized possession of it will be summarily dismissed from their posts and sent to work in the provinces.

Signed: First Secretary of the Central Committee of the CPSU."

The Americans Get Worried

At the White House, the President was pacing across the room.

"Look, this is the greatest challenge we've faced since the launch of the first Soviet Sputniks. What are the figures again?"

"GNP up 200 per cent this year, Sir," an aide began reciting. "Projected GNP growth rate based on present trends increasing up to 300 per cent per annum over the next five years. Our intelligence data indicate that actual defence expenditure is up by nearly 250 per cent since last year, even though the official figure remains the same. Consumer goods production has slightly decreased over the last year, even though wages have stayed the same or have increased, due to higher productivity. There are large increases in private savings, which the state can draw upon to carry out some of its projects, such as increased space exploration with a view to developing the Soviet Union's military potential in space."

"You see," the President looked reproachfully at his CIA aides, "I can understand you missing the Soviets infiltrating Africa for a couple of years... But this? What can we do now? Are we suddenly losing the economic and military race against the Soviets?" The President scrutinized silent faces around the room.

"However, I was told by my Chief Scientist that we can catch up with the Soviets anytime, if we really wanted to." He stopped pacing and sat down in his favorite armchair.

"Apparently, we already have all the information necessary to begin mass production of their drug, Socialin. We also have — and apparently have had for some years — both the necessary teaching personnel and the know-how as regards the meditation practice. Unfortunately, the Russians made off with one of the chief exponents of these techniques in the West. It seems incredible to me that for all these years we have neglected the warnings of our own experts about the necessity to develop a socially acceptable and safe pleasure-producing and healing drug.

"We must find the means for doing so now. We are grossly behind the Soviets. Some of the preliminary reports on drugs like LSD-25 which were produced at our request by the CIA and DARPA teams strike me as being impractical, expensive, and sociologically naive. It seems to me that our opponents have taken a more sophisticated and, at the same time, more hard-headed approach.

"Gentlemen, I would personally hate to see America follow Russia's lead for the second time in a decade. Our security, prestige, and our future are at stake. We must set to work immediately."

Holiday on the Black Sea

Anna was driving her new Moskvich along the twisting mountain road. Greenery on the side of the mountain, snow-capped peaks, rivers meandering deep down into the gorges — everything around her today gave her a feeling of purity and peace. She was glad to be going on a new assignment, which promised to be little more than a holiday on the Black Sea coast. She almost felt she was entitled to it after all the arduous weeks she had spent in Zambia. Traveling hundreds of miles along rough terrain, performing her undercover duties as a geologist with a Soviet team, and, on top of that, gathering intelligence, passing on instructions to local insurgents, drawing maps for the secret cachets of arms and equipment which were going to be dropped into the jungle. Somewhere along the line, despite all precautions, Anna had picked up a rare tropical disease from an insect bite, which took weeks to diagnose even after she had been flown back to Moscow. When she had recovered, Vlas called her in and gave her a new assignment.

The steep climb ended, and as soon as Anna reached the crest of the last hill, a breathtaking view of the Black Sea appeared before her, reaching far out to the horizon beyond the lush surrounding hills and mountains. She pulled over to the side of the road to admire the view and check her directions once more. She was on the right track: four kilometers past the Green Peninsula settlement, second turn, unmarked, to the left. Then, after about 100 yards, there should be a sign prohibiting entry and then a guard to whom she was to present her ID.

Anna had no difficulty finding the place. First, she passed through a bustling tourist settlement with hundreds of people milling between the beach and the promenade, lining up at drink stalls, sitting on park benches. Then, after a short drive along an unmarked but well-maintained road, she plunged into a world of silence, interrupted only by the sounds of birds and cicadas. She mused that most people, including the locals, probably did not even know where the road led to, and would not even bother to ask. This subtropical retreat was full of hideouts for top government officials and resorts for the KGB and the military. They were completely cut off from the rest of the population. Most of the people who served at these secret establishments were brought in from Moscow to eliminate the need to involve locals.

Anna passed the 'Entry Strictly Prohibited' sign. The guard came out from his hut and stopped the car. She showed her pass. He gave it a cursory glance — he had obviously been warned of her impending arrival — and waved her on. Anna got out of the car to open a wooden gate, which completely concealed the interior of the yard. She opened the gate and paused. It was just how she had imagined it. A small Mediterranean-style villa. Her rooms were on the first floor, so the view would be even better. The lawn was well-kept and citrus trees were in full blossom. An air of tranquility prevailed. There was no sign of life. "Like an enchanted place," she thought. But she knew better, of course. She craved for a break from her habitual suspiciousness.

Anna drove her car into the garage, and then walked around the garden. "Oh, even an arbor." Small but comfortable. Just the place for her to retreat to with one of her favorite volumes of poetry. Yes, she badly needed a break to recover. Experience had taught her that a volume of Pushkin, Rimbaud, or Robert Frost (she was fluent in English and French, as well as Russian) was almost a compulsory companion to the manual on the KGB procedures if she was to retain her sanity and carry on with her job till she would reach the pension age (or die somewhere in a lonely spot on one of her more dangerous assignments — the thought she liked to always push to the back of her mind).

Anna heard soft steps from behind. A tall man with a dark tan and a tuft of unruly blond hair was standing at the entrance to the arbor. "He hasn't changed that much," she thought. Usually, she reflected, people who have experienced what he must have gone through looked older. There was some uncustomary mellowness in his smile, but that was all.

"Good afternoon, Mr. Snowden," she greeted him in English.

"Good afternoon... Anna."

"Oh, you remember my name. You have an excellent memory."

"It is a prerequisite for my job, as it must be for yours."

Snowden came towards her and shook her hand.

"So, you came to smooth over my transition to a new persona?" he joked. "Anyhow, I'm glad; I didn't like that over-zealous little lieutenant who brought me here from Moscow."

"Well, you realize, of course," Anna sounded a little defensive, "that somebody in your position must have security protection and also have someone to liaise with Moscow. The medical specialists will still be coming here regularly as well to examine your progress."

"Oh, yes, I know," Richard, sighed resignedly. "I have the honor of being the first subject in the most extensive social experiment undertaken by the Party. Vlas already told me that. I guess my mind and my increasingly frail body," he smiled jauntily, if a little artificially, "now belong to the Party — and to science. I don't mind, as long as my spirit is left intact. I gather," he smiled enigmatically, "the experiment hasn't progressed that far yet?"

Anna smiled back but said nothing.

"You want to see some peach trees I have just planted?" He changed the subject. "I always wanted to plant some trees so I asked the gardener if I could help him. You know, we use trees for furniture, firewood, and all that — but very few people ever plant them. It doesn't seem fair. Anyhow, I found the act very gratifying."

"He sure has changed from that former uptight think-tank nerd," thought Anna. They went to a small orchard in the corner of the yard. Richard was obviously glad to have an English-speaking companion and was talking to Anna excitedly; she listened, smiling with a slight air of superiority and indulgence, as one would do with an over-enthusiastic child.

A few days passed. Anna felt more and more at home. They talked a bit, read a lot, listened to music. She taught Richard how to cook some Russian dishes, while he worked on improving her chess strategy. They could easily have passed for a couple holidaying on the Black Sea except that there they slept in separate bedrooms. Every evening Anna went to the phone to give her report to the Kremlin. Usually, it consisted of only a few sentences. There was little news from Moscow as well, except to tell her that a team of specialists would soon arrive to talk to Richard and take some fresh EEG recordings.

Occasionally, they drove to an isolated beach reserved for members of the secret police. They swam in the clear waters of the lagoon, separated by high fences from the outside world.

There were only half a dozen people on the beach — a few KGB officers with their languid wives, religiously acquiring a tan, regarded as a status symbol back in Moscow. In contrast, the surrounding beaches were so crowded that one could hardly see the sand among the sweating, heaving, seal-like sunburnt human forms. It was during one of these excursions that the monotonous, although pleasant course of their lives took a new turn.

Anna and Richard still treated each other with some reserve. Somewhere, in a dark, well-protected corner of Anna's consciousness, he was a foreign military expert who was also a witness to her escapade back in Bermuda. He also saw her as a person responsible for the deaths of innocent people for the sake of obeying the Party's orders. Although his new life and the surroundings had somewhat dulled the pain of separation from his past, the incident on the plane still occasionally flashed through his mind.

One afternoon, they stumbled upon an isolated lagoon surrounded by white sand dunes. Anna felt that these few weeks of rest had obviously perked up her physique. She swam far out to the sea, with Richard following her.

As they swam further on, Richard felt a strong pull of the undercurrent. They must have entered one of the rare rips off the coast.

"Go back!" he shouted.

Anna must have realized too they were being pulled out to sea and began to paddle furiously towards the beach. But neither of them made any progress. The current only took them further out.

Richard recalled something he must have read in a survival manual: do not fight the current. Go with it. If you are lucky, it will take you closer to the shore or at least you will retain strength to stay alive until help arrives.

"Just float! Do not fight the current," he shouted to Anna as she was getting desperate.

As they were being swept further to the sea, the current weakened. They must have entered deeper waters.

Richard waved his arms above his head and shouted. Anna joined him.

They were just floating now, maybe half a mile out to the sea.

Oh, blessed relief! Someone must have spotted them or heard them onshore. A motorboat sped towards them, with two lifesavers who heaved them onboard, disheveled but happy to be safe.

Anna's long hair was covering her face and she did not realize immediately that one of her breasts had slipped out of its bikini cup. The burly lifesavers ogled her anatomy avidly.

She noticed it and covered herself.

Richard looked aside pretending not to notice this little incident. The truth was that, for the first time since that fateful African debacle, he had again become aware of her as a woman.

They came home late and had some young Georgian wine, traditional spiced bread, and cheese for dinner and listened to a stereo recording of Carmina Burana, a favourite of Anna's.

Richard, still slightly euphoric from their brief encounter with danger began talking about his experience of spiritual renewal, and his present contentment despite the virtual imprisonment.

He was animated and passionate describing his experience with Socialin, and scathing about the stupidity of the authorities who wanted to harness something as nebulous as "enlightenment" to their pragmatic goals of rising productivity and fighting drunkenness and drug addiction.

Anna had to confess that on this particular occasion she found his enthusiasm strangely attractive. Even his rave against Vlas and the authorities did not sound too far-reaching to her.

The sincerity and ardor of Richard's story was in such vivid contrast to the drunken "confessions" of some of the men she knew, both Russian and foreign, who were either cynical and pessimistic or boastful and insincere.

Richard got up and poured some more wine.

"Are you trying to get me drunk or something," Anna protested jokingly. She really was getting tipsy and felt vague stirrings of sexual desire, blaming music and wine for it.

Maybe it was this sense of relief from danger, or the tranquil days they had spent together, that made the difference. Maybe it was the strange aura of calm and contentment that was emanating from the 'new' Richard. Anna was drawn to the strong swimmer who did not lose his cool in danger.

Anna did not have to worry about the incompatibility of her duty with sexual intimacy. Vlas had informed her before that there were no constraints in her personal relationship with Richard. He was a great believer in gathering every bit of information about people in his custody and was an even stronger believer in the fact that some of the most sensitive information is often procured in bed.

To Anna, this confusion between the supposedly most personal aspect of her life and the call of duty had long ceased to be bewildering or unsettling.

With harshness that comes from battered life and childhood, she considered herself frigid and learned to disassociate herself completely from her feelings, imitating — very successfully, she was told — the sexual orgasm of the passionate variety usually portrayed in books and movies for the benefit of ignorant men (and most men were totally ignorant about woman's real sexual desires and feelings, she felt). She had made some of her most fruitful intelligence scoops in that manner. She was recorded in Vlas's unofficial listing as one of the most experienced KGB 'swallows'. Anna felt she had never been in love and came to regard the whole concept of love as a bit of romantic nonsense.

"Ah, it's all wine and music. He is still just a nerd and at least half an enemy of the people," she thought lazily, sipping the Georgian *Saperayi*. The KGB buyers certainly knew their *vino*. It must have been at least ten years old, although once she tasted a fifty-year-old *Saperayi* at a government banquet in Moscow.

Richard in the meantime was feeling emboldened by Anna's lascivious frame spread on the couch, glass of wine in hand, eyeing him with what he interpreted as a far from hostile gaze. He remembered reading something about prisoners getting attracted to their captors (or was it *vice versa?*) Almost all his feelings and experiences seemed to derive from something he had read somewhere, accompanied usually by a precise reference down to the title and page.

He held out his hand to her and opened it playfully. On his palm lay a small red pill. "It's Socialin," he said. "Have you tried it? By the way, it can act a bit of an aphrodisiac." This was a blatant lie that he had just concocted.

Anna at first reacted with mock shock.

"Me? No, I cannot drink or take drugs on the job. Well, not to the point that they will begin to cloud my judgment..."

"Half the country is taking this thing... quite officially," Richard persevered.

He could see Anna wavering in her resolve. He did not know (although he could guess if he strained his imagination, which he was not in the mood to) that in the course of her duties she sometimes smoked pot or took a bit of hash or coke and occasionally even stranger concoctions that her clients shared with her. Her only rule was that the secrets she was going to ferret out were bigger than the ones she could blurt out. And that the man (and it was almost always the men she was working with) was the usual variety "sitting duck", like a diplomat or a scientist and not some double-dealing Colonel Abel who could outwit, outsmoke, and out-coke her.

Sometimes, it was a close call, she had to admit to herself.

Would she gain extra trust from Richard if she cooperated now? Yes, it looked that way. Would he tell Vlas? No.

She smiled, "I suppose I need to understand what it is that the whole country is hooked on, at least for the purposes of my job."

"A call of duty, nothing more, as Vlas would have said," Richard imitated Vlas' gruff accent.

She swallowed the red pill and washed it down with more wine. In a minute, she felt a strange sensation which she could only describe like utter closeness to Richard, and not only to Richard but to everything in her immediate vicinity and yes, even the world at large. Yes, even the planets far above. She looked in his eyes and could swear that he felt like a long-lost brother she never had. Waves of affection washed over her. Her heart was opened and aflutter with new, gentler beats.

"It feels so... so... good..." was all she could mutter.

Even the room they were in felt like magic to her. The paintings on the wall became alive, the softly swaying trees outside whispered to her, the gentle murmur of the sea was meant for her and Richard alone.

Upstairs in Richard's room she felt as if she was continually rising toward orgasm, hovering at that point between pleasure and pain. She had to do something to release herself from this sweet torture — cry, laugh, dig her nails into his back. She found herself crying and laughing alternatively. At first she wanted to shift into her usual 'swallow' mode, a competent seductress who knew exactly what to do to make men enjoy sex. But Richard held her tightly, as if he knew what was happening with her, caressing her softly.

She felt Richard's hands touching her skin and whispering softly into her ear, "You are free now."

She had the first real orgasm of her life with Richard that night. The next morning, an awkward silence prevailed over breakfast until Richard asked Anna why she had never taken Socialin before. Well, she said, rather matter-of-factly, people in her position were not allowed to take it. Vlas looked down upon even those who practiced meditation alone, which was officially permitted. He felt especially mistrustful about it when it came to his close subordinates. He liked to say that he knew how every KGB agent ticked, inside and outside.

"Is he afraid that he would no longer be able to control his agents if they took Socialin?" Richard wanted to know. Anna did not comment. She felt at peace with herself and Vlas' preoccupations seemed very remote to her now.

He explained to her the tranquility he felt when he meditated with Socialin, how it pervaded his whole being, how he felt a feeling of oneness with the universe, a quiet sense of ecstasy. It was much better taken together, he explained. The pill only opened the gates of paradise, the meditation kept the door opened and let the stars in.

"Well, then why have sex at all?" Anna asked half-jokingly. "Isn't it true that most mystics were celibates, and what you are describing to me now sounds like a fully-fledged mystical experience?"

Richard had thought of that too, but he felt that the anti-sexual slant of the traditional church teachings was caused by thousands of years of propaganda by frustrated clerics who knew nothing of true mystical experience. The feeling of bliss he had experienced as he became more advanced in his meditation became vastly different from the pleasure of orgasm. It was accompanied by a sensation of total inner stillness. He felt that the two experiences were not mutually exclusive, and could be combined if one practiced enough (which the saints were not allowed to by the Church, for obvious reasons).

"I am sure you have heard of Tantra yoga," Richard queried. Yes, she had heard about it and even read some old books in translation. But she found it to be too abstruse, too convoluted. She found that the illustrated copy of Kama Sutra that they gave her at the spy school was much more to the point and far more useful.

During the next few days, their frankness with each other deepened as they told each other the stories of their lives. Her experience with Richard had freed her from the habitual caution she felt with outsiders and especially with men. After taking the pill that Richard shared, Anna became playful and more jovial. Her dreams became sweet and peaceful, full of erotic imagery and unfamiliar scenes of her wandering inside ancient castles, looking for hidden treasures. At times, she felt almost in love with Richard for what he had done to help her.

Anna noticed that Richard, in between their little frolics, would withdraw into the arbor and work feverishly on some papers. When she asked him what it was, he answered, "I feel a compulsion to solve an old mathematical puzzle that I have been working on for years."

One day, Anna peeked into Richard's notes. Dozens of pages of his notebook were covered with complicated formulas and calculations. She knew that Vlas would become suspicious if her reports contained nothing more than descriptions of their walks and casual dinner conversations. There had to be some tangible "intelligence" to justify her presence here.

She photographed Alfred's scribbles that were totally incomprehensible to her and sent the film to Moscow, expecting to hear nothing but the usual, "Keep watching him." But a few days later she received a phone call from Vlas. He instructed her to return to Moscow immediately, as her ward was to be put under the care of the Ministry of Defence, not the KGB.

"Our experts are very, very excited about his notes and think he can now be of much greater use to them than before," Vlas told her. "He had produced some real scientific breakthroughs that have far-reaching military implications," he confided to her, sounding almost respectful. He thanked Anna for her good work.

"What's he actually working on?" Anna tried to use one of the rare moments when Vlas was open to questions.

"Oh, I'm not exactly sure myself. Something about laser beam generation."

"Hmmm," mumbled Anna disappointedly, as Vlas hung up.

Her Black Sea holiday was obviously over. Laser beams were more important to Vlas than cosmic beams.

When they were saying goodbye, Richard took out a packet of red pills from his drawer and gave it to her. "Take this," he said, "nobody will ever know. You need to take them for a while, together with the meditation, for the full effect to take hold."

She slipped the container in her pocket and kissed him softly on the cheek. "Good bye, my little guru," she whispered. "Don't get too saintly, please. I want to practice a little Tantra with you next time."

In her mind she doubted that there ever will be the next time. Vlas had other plans for her, she was sure.

The Conspirators

The basement flat was poorly lit, and it was difficult to make out anyone's face. At short intervals there would be a knock at the end of a long corridor and a new person would bring with him a cloud of frosty air and the fresh smell of recently fallen snow. They vigorously brushed the snow off their boots, as if respect for their host's floor somehow reflected the solemnity of the cause which had brought them there.

The person who showed visitors into the darkened room was a post-graduate student, courteous to a fault, but with brisk and impatient movements betokening a fiery temperament. Finally, he led in the last visitor, a tall man with roughly-hewn features, clumsy and ill at ease, wearing cheap imitation leather boots of the kind worn in villages, but with workers' overalls underneath an ill-fitting padded jacket.

Inside the room, the guests were introduced to a bearded man with fiery, although somewhat furtive gaze, whom the student called Grigory. He had the suave manner of a public relations man or a with-it university lecturer. He motioned everyone present to take their seats, introducing them to each other only by their first names. "Nikolai... Lubomir... Timofei..." As the last visitor was seated, Grigory began to speak, ensconcing himself deeply into the armchair, as if to hide even from the scant light illuminating the room.

"Comrades, friends... this is the first but hopefully not the last meeting we are having. The person who brought you into this room, my dear friend and associate, Pavel, has been the primary contact for all of you until now. I can assure you that your identities and your words here will remain absolutely confidential. It is I, if anyone, with the sensitive position that I occupy, who stands to lose the most from any disclosure," he said with solemnity.

He looked around and let a pregnant pause hang in the air as if to convince everyone that the loss of prestige and power that he could suffer would indeed be considerable.

"But," he added, "There is some good news, too. We are aware that in the government itself, even in its highest circles, there are people who are against the new reforms and would do almost anything to stop them from spreading.

"However, we must not limit ourselves to talking, we must do something. We must create a nucleus of resistance to the changes that are sweeping the country. Even though they seem to be embraced by the short-sighted and the unprincipled among the masses, we are aware that a great number of people are also ready to resist them."

"I agree with you," said Nikolai, a dark-haired man in a military jacket, which he must have picked up in a second-hand store. "The high ideals of our society are being betrayed by the Party, who have decided to pander to the lowest pleasure-seeking instincts in the masses rather than elevate them to their true status worthy of Communists. Many of my friends feel the same way. We sometimes meet at my place and have a drink of the old-fashioned vodka — which, by the way, is becoming more and more difficult to obtain — and talk about the old days and the battles and hardships we went through. Back then, hardships were not impediments to progress, but a challenge. If we don't do something about this soon our nation will become a nation of soft-hearted and soft-bodied pleasure seekers.

"Our leaders seem contented to reap the benefits of increased productivity without thinking about the price we have to pay for it. Like the loss of nerve and moral fibre, and the willingness to repel foreign aggression at any cost."

"Thank you, Comrade Nikolai, I think you expressed, rather succinctly, thoughts we all share," said Grigory, brushing his hair back with a slightly theatrical gesture.

"But if we are to make any impact at all, we need both organization and money. We are fortunate to have with us here today Father Timofei, who has a great deal of influence in Russian Orthodox Church and who promises to provide us with the financial support necessary to put our movement on a proper footing."

Father Timofei, a small plump man with a bulbous face, triangular beard, and a pleasant singsong voice, moved forward in his chair.

"Yes, this is true. Many people in the Church are greatly alarmed by the changes taking place. It is true that we have had to work under unfavourable conditions before, what with the State preventing us from propagating our beliefs while it indulged, unhindered, in scurrilous anti-religious propaganda.

"But even in our demoralized society, we still had people who realized the sinfulness of their lives and who came to us for solace and confession. The reformed alcoholics, the people who committed atrocities in war or during the purges, those who were simply crushed by the meaninglessness of their materialistic lives, the young and the idealistic as well as the old and tradition-conscious — they all came to us as a last resort. But now, the understanding of the sinfulness of humanity and its need for redemption is disappearing," Father Timofei blew his nose with a trumpeting crescendo, as if to underscore the gravity of the loss that his nation was suffering.

"It is true that people no longer drink quite as much. They also tell me that this new-fangled meditation business — which I can tell you authoritatively is nothing more than a pagan and inferior version of Christian prayer — makes frivolous people forget their sinful deeds and therefore deprives them of the feeling of guilt, so beneficial for the soul, especially when it is accompanied by the Lord's forgiveness, administered by one of his servants.

"So what appears to be a good change on the surface — the superficial cheerfulness, the reduction in inner turmoil and social disharmony, is actually nothing more than the temptation of the Devil to forget one's inherent sinfulness, to lapse into the mortal man's hubris of imagining himself equal to God or the saints. What else? There are some disturbing signs that this indeed may be the work of Lucifer... While we notice that church attendance in general has dwindled substantially, we get occasional visits from one of these new converts, his mind distorted by this horrendous drug, this so-called 'Socialin'." Father Timofei was almost choking with indignation when he said the name of drug, carrying for him the double whammy of the Communist dogma and the pagan or even otherworldly temptation.

"They speak with the assurance of the False Prophets and claim the sort of mystical experience reserved to our revered saints. They attempt to translate the beautiful esoteric messages of the faith into the crude vernacular, saying that our books are obsolete and divorced from life," Father Timofei sounded now almost on the verge of tears, frequently blowing his nose and touching his bushy brows with the handkerchief.

"I tell you, what a half century of anti-religious propaganda and persecution have failed to accomplish, these new reforms, unthinkingly supported by the government, soon will. The Orthodox Church will be destroyed! And with it will disappear forever that glorious part of our heritage, which Great Russian writers and poets have drawn upon in the past for the benefit of all humanity. Surely we will not let this happen!" Father Nikolai raised his sonorous voice to a higher pitch. "All people who value tradition and custom, authority and obedience, should rebel against this ungodly scheme. My organization and I will make it our task to destroy this diabolical connivance which would deprive the people of their only chance of true redemption."

Grigory noticed that the worker was fidgeting in his chair, impatient to comments. "Yes, friend," he motioned him to speak.

"Well, to be frank," he began in a stumbling voice, "I don't understand too much about sin and redemption, but I do know that the lives of some honest workers, who, like myself, do not want to follow the crowd, are being made unbearable. Sure, there is no official pressure to take Socialin or practice meditation. But we've found that ever since the stuff was introduced into our factory, there has been loads of indirect pressure to go along with the new reform. As more and more workers toed the line in taking the drug, productivity did climb, it's true, but with it also climbed the norms demanded by the government. In the past, we were able to avoid this by slacking on the job, by using out-of-date technology, or even plain sabotage. Even though we never had an effective trade union movement in our country, we were able to put pressure on those who tried to do better than the rest and therefore hold productivity at a level that could be managed by ordinary folk like me without undue strain. In the meantime, we increased our wages by pilfering factory goods and moonlighting; you know the things we all do.

"Now it's all changed. The people who were the greatest loafers now work like crazy after they've taken that drug. You can't cope with the pace they set and that makes us, the true supporters of the workers' rights, seem like lazy bums, almost saboteurs. Yet my friends and me — we want none of this goddamn stuff. I don't know what it feels like to take it, but I sure don't want to slave my guts out like some of those fools... No thanks... It's not for me."

"Lubomir, and what do you say?" Grigory addressed the last visitor. "You are a geologist by profession, I believe?"

"Yes, that's right," Lubomir's voice was coarse and loud. "And I tell you, when this new craze spreads throughout the country, I will take a long journey to one of the most remote forests I have been to during my work, and stay there. I don't want to follow the herd as it is led to the slaughterhouse, or wherever. I never did. I think there are ways of making oneself happy other than swallowing some pills and repeating a nonsense word. I get my highs from nature, from going for a swim in a rushing mountain stream when the weather is hot, or from reading a good book by the fire when the weather is cold. I play my guitar when I'm blue or lonely. I work hard without any Socialin, harder than any of the guys that take it... And... I'm happy the way I am. That's all."

Pavel, the student, went out into the corridor briefly, and upon return, whispered something into Grigory's ear.

"Friends," Grigory's voice had a note of urgency in it, "we must terminate our meeting now, but I can assure you that your words have made me even more determined to pursue our cause. Please take note of all the other people in your vicinity or place of employment who are like-minded and give their names and addresses to Pavel. He's our specialist in conspiratorial techniques" — Pavel raised his hand appreciatively — "and he will screen the people, just as you have been screened, to exclude any possible agent provocateurs. We hope we will have many more people at our next meeting when we will discuss practical organizational and financial matters. Good luck until then, and please, leave one by one."

Pavel looked outside once more to make sure that the coast was clear and beckoned the first visitor to leave.

On the way out, he whispered to each of them the new meeting place and the new password.

The whirling snow swallowed their figures as they disappeared into the night.

Democracy in Action

"So you think his discovery may have some practical applications?"

Glavny's voice, after it had passed through a scrambler, became even raspier and quiet almost to the point of being inaudible. "You think it might give a clear-cut first-strike capability over the Americans?"

"Good, very good," he confirmed after hearing the reply, "just keep interrogating him along those lines; make sure you bleed the guy of anything he is still hiding. You've got a *carte blanche* from me."

He put the receiver down and smiled one of his rare smiles that made his wrinkly and craggy face look like that of an old and aged baboon, with his bushy and protruding eyebrows emphasizing the effect.

He, and not only he, but also all of his predecessors had been waiting a long time for this moment. To be the ruler of the most powerful nation on Earth! And what's more, to be the ruler of a happy nation! And still remain under the banner of Communism! This was beyond his wildest dreams — perhaps not beyond those of the idealistic dreamers of the past like Marx and Lenin — but certainly beyond the dreams of practical politicians like Stalin and himself.

Glavny could now prove to the world, for example, that Socialist agriculture does work. He would have to, of course, subsidize it even more heavily, but what the hell? Now he could afford it, what with the massive increase in industrial productivity. He smiled gleefully at the idea of Soviet merchant vessels loaded with golden Ukrainian grain leaving, practically for the first time since the Revolution, for foreign, maybe even American, ports. That would be the ultimate insult, the ultimate humiliation to the haughty, fat-bellied capitalists!

He recalled his drunken conversation with Vlas not so long ago. He was raving about the wealth of the nation that they could create with more productive and sober masses. But Vlas corrected him. "Ultimate power always lies in strength. Not in wealth or influence, or, God forbid, ideas, but in brute, naked force. Since times immemorial, force has ruled the world." And Glavny had to agree with Vlas, the old, pragmatic fox that he was. Russia's favourite poet, Pushkin, put it so tersely and so beautifully; even Glavny could not improve on it:

"I will buy everything," said the Gold.
"And I will take everything,"
Answered the Sword.

Glavny rose from his chair and paced briskly across his study. Perhaps too briskly, for his face soon became contorted with pain. "Those blasted piles!" he thought angrily. Even after three operations carried out by the best Moscow specialists, they still hurt occasionally.

He pulled out a square, brown box from his pocket and looked at it with consternation. Another forty whole minutes before the time lock would click and allow him to smoke another cigarette. Those tyrant doctors, constantly threatening him with a stroke! He threw the box on the desk, and after a few moments, reached, looking quite guilty, around the corner of the bookshelf. It was not his favourite *Sobranie*, just a plain *Kazbek* pack left there for him by the ever-solicitous Vlas. But it was good enough at a moment like this. He lit the cigarette and drew in the smoke deeply, with an expression of intense pleasure. By the time he had finished his secret stash, the lock on the box would be nearly ready to open. He felt almost as excited as when, many decades ago, he stole his first cigarette from his father.

The guard's voice boomed through the intercom: "Comrade Bur is waiting at the Reception."

"Let him in," said Glavny softly, still enjoying the slight dizziness produced by the untimely cigarette. Vlas walked in, looking excited. "Good news, Glavny... great news," he almost shouted at the door. He was the only person who was allowed to call Glavny by his nickname.

"The Defence people are saying that the calculations of that guy, Snowden, are far more advanced than anything they've ever seen or done themselves. They think they can now cut production time for a prototype anti-missile laser beam weapon down to a few months. He's come up with some really new, fantastic ideas on energy generation and beam concentration."

"I know all that," Glavny liked to put his subordinates down occasionally. "I've just spoken to Defence myself. But tell me what's going on in the provinces."

Vlas's face clouded over. He wanted to save that piece of news for last. But obviously Glavny had already heard something, so he had to spit it out.

"Well," he said, "productivity is continuing to rise throughout the country. The harvest in Kazakhstan was finished two weeks earlier than usual and with virtually no losses, despite negative climatic conditions. It made me realize," he remarked, "that previously we must have been losing up to twenty per cent of our harvest through sheer negligence and inefficiency."

"All right, all right," Glavny did not like to dwell on past mistakes. "What other news do you have?"

He must already know, thought Vlas, bracing himself for the worst. "We also have disturbing reports coming up from some regions, Glavny... we may not have foreseen all the social consequences of our project."

"What reports, what unforeseen consequences?" Glavny's eyes narrowed to slit.

"Well, it is really difficult to evaluate these reports, so I had to travel to a couple of places myself to see what was going on."

"And what is going on?"

"It appears that people in many enterprises and even entire provinces are showing more initiative in running their own affairs that the local authorities did not anticipate. It's funny, Glavny," Vlas sounded slightly amused, "but this is something we've been bleating about for years. 'Worker participation', 'citizen action', 'voluntary labor', you know all that crap. Only now, it's not just a showpiece — it's for real. And the authorities are finding it a little hard to handle, to say the least.

"Here are some facts: In Dnieprodzerzhinsk, your home town, of all places, workers from a local factory, in their own free time, planted a green belt around the factory to prevent pollution from reaching their settlement. As it happened, the zone that they used was intended for factory expansion. They also introduced recycling methods which promise to virtually eliminate domestic and industrial waste they had been drowning in. The factory management did not even have time to intervene, it happened so fast. Ordinarily, it would have taken weeks just to round up some 'volunteers'."

Glavny was listening impassively after reaching for another cigarette and lighting it. This was unexpected but nothing that he would lose too much sleep over.

"Next," Vlas continued, "in the city of Novosibirsk, local residents have decided to improve their food supply and have opened a large cooperative with its own greenhouses, fish breeding tanks, supplies for home gardens, etc. The result is almost complete self-sufficiency, which has forced the closure of many government stores."

That was a bit more worrisome, Glavny thought, but still not revolutionary. So some stores will close but as long as workers continued turning up for their work at their factories every morning, who cares?

"In the city of Gorky, worker participation in management and production at a car factory has reached such proportions that the management is practically isolated and has to go to workers' meetings simply to find out what is going on."

"So?" Glavny stubbed out his cigarette. "What's wrong with that? I agree that this business of 'democracy in action' may be a little excessive, but I don't see anything drastically wrong with it. The production quotas are not suffering, are they? There is no violence. And if a few bureaucrats have to shift their asses around a little more, so what? I always wanted something like this to happen. A good old shake-them-up. Of course, it would have been better if it would have come directly from our own initiatives."

"Unfortunately," Vlas continued, "the reaction of some of those bureaucrats was quite unexpected. In a word, they decided that 'if you can't beat them, join them'. Here is the list of government and Party officials who, in spite of our secret decree, have resorted to the combined use of meditation and Socialin."

He put a thick pile of papers on Glavny's desk. Glavny leafed through them, occasionally calling out the names, "Ostroborodhov, Tikhonov, Mazur... I don't believe it, old, hardened Communists, comrades-in-arms, close friends... hundreds of them."

Glavny's fingers were trying to pry open his cigarette case. Vlas, who knew that it would not open yet, reached into his own pocket, handed Glavny a golden-tipped *Sobranie* and quickly lit it.

"What do you think, Vlas?" Glavny took a long draw and leaned back in his chair. "Maybe we got more than we bargained for, eh?" He became engrossed in his thoughts for a moment. "What if you and I were the only ones left who didn't take the goddamn stuff? Do you think we could still keep things under control?"

Vlas kept silent. From his long experience, he knew that it was better not to pipe in with any suggestions when Glavny was thinking aloud, even when he asked for suggestions.

"You know," Glavny's voice was surprisingly calm, "I don't think we could, I mean keep things under our control... but," his voice assumed that steely tone which Vlas was so familiar with, "we'll make damn sure that we will do all we can, while we can."

He pressed a Dictaphone button on his desk and started to dictate in that stumbling, sparse, simplistic but at the same time precise way that was his hallmark. The hacks downstairs will correct the grammar and all that.

"To all members of central government bodies, heads of Party organizations, top KGB and military personnel:

"The unauthorized possession and use of Socialin in conjunction with meditation will, from today, be punishable by the death penalty. A special unit will be formed under the direct supervision of Comrade V. Bur to insure the effectiveness of this new measure. You are encouraged to report to him any misconduct by your colleagues. Signed, First Secretary."

Vlas smirked contentedly. He had known all along that this crazy project would backfire. Now he was on familiar ground. He would show those blissed-out idiots who were the rulers in this country. They had played this 'democracy' charade long enough. The kid gloves were coming off and underneath them were the iron fists of the Party and the KGB.

He smiled to himself, thinking his most secret thought: "Masses remain masses and we are the new elite, and the twain shall never meet."

Bigger Than an H-Bomb

"Call in the monk," Vlas gave the order to a KGB lieutenant. Snowden noted that Vlas's tone had changed a great deal since he had seen him a couple of months ago. He now sounded totally self-confident and in command of the situation.

The door opened and a bearded man in a green military uniform without epaulettes walked in. Snowden gasped. It was Swami. He was about to ask him about his strange garb but Swami pre-empted his question.

"When in Rome, do as the Romans do," he chuckled easily. "It's better in this clime, too." Richard wondered what Swami had been through in the past few months.

Vlas impatiently indicated to Swami to sit down and began talking bluntly through his lieutenant, who translated.

"Gentlemen, your services are much needed and appreciated by the Party and the government. We have achieved a great deal, but some serious obstacles remain. Unfortunately, we are still surrounded by enemies who do not want to see our system progress and prosper. Therefore, we still need weapons to guard against their evil designs. And, to invent such weapons, we need people with superior intelligence. We are very impressed with the quality of the work that Mr Snowden has produced recently..."

"It was just doodling, something to do with my time," interjected Snowden. "I didn't want to be idle, and this was the most complicated problem that I ever worked on..."

"That's fine with us," laughed Vlas. "Just do some more of your doodling. Our experts have told me that your humble efforts will save us months, maybe even years, in developing a viable laser beam weapon system."

"And now," he addressed himself to Swami, "I remember you saying that your meditation technique increases intelligence and creativity, and that you are also in possession of some advanced techniques which could help an individual to become more creative and intelligent?"

"That is correct," said Swami.

"Right," Vlas sounded as if he was giving orders to his lieutenant to have his uniform dry-cleaned for the parade. "I want you to do everything you can to increase this bright boy's intelligence even further."

He waved his hand towards Snowden. "We want our Army, Air Force, and the Navy to become invincible. We are no longer contented to live under the capitalist sword of Damocles, and the threat of Mutually Assured Destruction. We want the whole world to see that our system is superior to every other, in every respect. In other words, we want the assurance of the unilateral destruction of our enemies, and our own survival in case of an all-out war."

Snowden looked at Swami. He did not expect his dabbling with what he felt was a purely scientific problem, in which he had engaged primarily to take his mind off Anna, who he knew was soon to depart from him, to have such repercussions.

He waited for Swami to say something. He did not feel very much like helping Vlas and the cause of Communism. Of course, he could not refuse outright, that would be too dangerous. But he could keep on doodling for months on end without producing anything really worthwhile. The heights of scientific inspiration are, like those of God designs, unfathomable.

Snowden could not believe his ears when he heard Swami speak. "To make your country invincible appears to be an admirable goal. This is one way of stopping the war and violence that prevails in the world. I'll do anything I can to make the people of your country strong."

"That's the kind of talk I like!" Vlas said jubilantly. "No ifs and buts and convoluted arguments!" He rose from his chair. "Gentlemen, we have no time to lose. I will let you discuss your plans, and then I expect Mr Snowden to start working as soon as possible with our crack team from the Ministry of Defence. Goodbye gentlemen — and good luck."

Richard and Swami were left alone in the room.

"Well," Richard said, looking at Swami quizzically, "I don't know how you feel about it, but the idea of helping them to design weapons that may be used to destroy my people does not appeal to me."

"There is no such thing as 'my people'. Mankind is one."

"Yes, I agree in theory," Richard retorted, "but I can't help disagreeing with you in this instance. Especially when someone like Vlas is trying to use me... I think I'll just sit on the fence and pretend to be doing something without producing any results."

"Inaction is inimical to life. Maybe you can think," Swami smiled one of his most mischievous smiles, "with all your newly-found creativity, you can design weapons in such a way that they work as it is supposed to work when the decisive time comes? People like Vlas and Glavny would not know the difference."

"Yes, but people like Colonel Popov at the Defence may."

"Do not fear. Colonel Popov is on the same track as us. Nature acts through all of us. When you are at one with nature, with evolution, you cannot do wrong and cannot commit sins through your actions."

Snowden looked at him with growing mistrust.

"This may sound good in the Bhagavad Gita and may even work in chess, but in real life one can commit sins, like betraying one's country and helping the destruction of the world. What guarantee do I have that you are right and that Colonel Popov is 'on the same wavelength' as you and me? Frankly, I have great doubts about that."

"Being one with nature is not a matter of wishful thinking, that much I can tell you now. It is a matter of gradual transformation of mind and body — real, physical transformation. What you have been doing until now has been the beginning of that process. If you wish, I can teach you how to make it go faster. But you must give up that drug, Socialin. It served its purpose. Once the path through the jungle is made, there is no need to use the hatchet. There are some broken branches to pick up. This is the price you'll have to pay for what you see as your fast 'progress'."

"Yes, but you have not answered my question," Richard insisted. "If I'm not responsible for my actions, then all is justified — greed, violence, torture. We can blame fate, or karma, or natural law for everything..." Richard was becoming visibly excited.

Swami gave him a long look. "The feeling of responsibility for your actions is also part of nature, part of your mental makeup. It is not of your own choice. The sources of order and disorder are waging a constant battle, not only in every human and animal society, but also in the universe at large. You know, God, or evolution, if you prefer, operate in inscrutable ways. A criminal will murder a child and will be killed in return; but a savage will kill his child in time of famine, and survive to bring another child into the world. At this point in history, greed and violence seem to serve their masters well. Vlas and Glavny can tell you a great deal about this. But very soon, they may not. They are trapped in their own evil ways, and they had to call upon higher powers and higher knowledge to get them out of their predicament. This is where we and the Nature come in," Swami laughed infectiously, like a child delighted with the new possibilities in the game he was playing.

"But how do I know that I am one with nature? Every criminal and maniac can claim the same."

Swami thought for a moment and looked at Richard intently, as if wanting to see if he was ready to understand. "You will know that when the center from which you act becomes identical with the innermost point of your being, which is totally without desire and totally tranquil. Then you will have no doubts."

"Yes, yes," Richard continued, hardly listening to Swami's words. "But wouldn't this excuse be used by every passing maniac in history to justify his or her actions, however abominable? Who is to check on the false pretenders?"

Swami pondered a reply. "The knowledge I am talking about is like a strong medicine. True, in the wrong hands, it will become a poison. But humans have never had a shortage of poisons to carry out their intentions. We are not going to take this beautiful medicine off the shelf because it has the potential for abuse by False Pretenders. I agree that this knowledge must not fall into the hands of the ignorant. Reasonable precautions must be taken," he paused momentarily, "the medicine will be given not over the counter, but through a prescription, which we call initiation."

"Alright," Richard replied rather heatedly. He was getting irritated again by Swami's seeming irrationality and the obscurity of his intentions.

"Say, I know in the deepest recesses of my consciousness that I am tranquil and without desire and therefore incapable of incurring sin. How will other people know? How will they be able to tell the true claimant from the false?"

"Evolution will tell — in time. Order and harmony will ultimately prevail. But," Swami's eyes twinkled with a humorous sparkle, "I must say that if humans get impatient to know sooner, they will have to use a machine like the one invented by the Russians to distinguish the true claimant from the false one. Lack of desire is not a thought, it is a definite state of mind and body that can be measured and quantified if your equipment is sufficiently sophisticated and you know what to look for."

Swami saw that Richard was far from being reassured by his arguments.

"There will always be violence and disorder, and medicines will be used as poison, and scientific equipment will be used for reaffirming the false prophets' claims. But finally, the forces of order and harmony will assert themselves and establish a new balance. Life always triumphs over death, at least in our human realm, and at least for this stretch of the cosmic age."

"All right, let us presume for the moment that you are right and that there is some invisible hand of nature guiding us all toward some sort of perfection or harmony, rather than the destruction of the world," Richard decided to play along with Swami, although he was far from being convinced by him.

"Can you tell me now what I am supposed to do?" Richard made himself appear bewildered by the wealth of information he had received.

"I cannot tell you what to do. In time, you will know yourself. What I can do is to teach you a more clever way of withdrawing from the field of doing into the field of being. Then you will become established in the field of being. And from that field, you'll act. In your meditations you must have already had a glimpse of that field of being and of oneness with the universe. I can show you how to make it more permanent."

That suited Richard just fine. He was going to make the decision on the basis of his own progress in meditation and his own thinking.

"Show me," said Richard quietly, his agitation finally subsiding.

Swami leaned towards Richard and whispered a few words into his ear.

"Is that all?" Richard looked up to Swami in utter surprise.

"Yes, it is that small... and that big."

"But it seems like some sort of a trick..."

"Putting fertilizer into the soil is also a trick, and so is shattering a vase with a musical note. Just wait. This 'trick' can be more profound than the effects of an H-bomb," he added with his usual enigmatic smile.

A Report to the President from the Secretary of Department of Defence on the Progress of Project Counterbalance:

The M.I.T. team, together with specialists from the Pentagon, has finally developed a technique that seems to be in many ways superior to that used by the Russians. They have also created a drug that is at least five times more powerful than Socialin and is still completely side-effect-free. This drug, in combination with the memory and intelligence-enhancing substances that we have been working on before Project Counterbalance was initiated, gave us a most powerful tool for affecting not only motivation, but also the intellectual performance of an individual. A senior scientist who consented to be a research subject has just produced a major breakthrough in the seemingly deadlocked new weapon system utilizing ionising radiation from space. Relatively soon, this will give us a clear-cut first-strike capability over the Russians. In the meantime, we advise the State Department to adopt a much firmer stand in their negotiations with the Russians over their possible military alliance with the Chinese.

Signed, Secretary, Department of Defence

Glavny's Dream

Glavny shouted one of those elaborate oaths he had learned in the army. Those bastard Yanks! As if it wasn't enough for them to put a wedge between Russia and China, or to bribe the silly Chinks with their trade and secret promises of help in case of attack by the Russians. Now they're trying to blackmail him, Glavny! And when? Now, when the chances of patching up the most painful rift in the history of the Communist movement were the greatest.

The Great Helmsman has departed — let his body and soul rot in hell. The eternal delinquent, the proponent of 'perpetual revolution' is finally, gratefully, dead. Mao called any progress towards stability 'revisionism'. Mao tried to prevent the elite of China from becoming more powerful, more affluent, and more secure. Mao was struggling against the tide of nature, of man himself. "And why..." Glavny smirked, "...just because the poor bastard had a bullying father." Mao constantly struggled to dismantle, to renew the authority, even the authority he set up himself with his closest cronies.

Glavny remembered reading a secret report on the Chairman's psychological profile. It said that if Mao had been born fifty years before his time, he would probably have ended up in jail as a common criminal. All the traits — early separation from an authoritarian father, unbounded pride combined with rebelliousness, identification with fictional male heroes, acceptance of violence as a means to an end — pointed in that direction. But the 'historical situation' was such that a potential delinquent and a criminal with psychopathic tendencies was instead predestined to become the greatest revolutionary leader of the most populous nation on Earth.

Glavny recalled reading the secret report about Mao's shenanigans with virgin peasant girls in the very corridors of Communist power. That bastard never even treated his gonorrhea, infecting hundreds of innocent women.

Anyhow, the delinquent was now dead. It was no use to indulge in recriminations and analysis.

Was Glavny so angry with the Chairman because he secretly envied his power to inflict his dream — or his delusion — upon hundreds of millions of people so profoundly, and without any punishment?

Glavny sighed. He was born into a different 'historical situation', where social delinquents could no longer rise to supreme positions but had to satisfy themselves with menial jobs in the Secret Police. This was because the chief delinquent — Stalin — had been at the helm, and past delinquents make very authoritarian leaders when they get older. The men who rose to power in the shadow of the Father of the Nation had to distinguish themselves, as Glavny did, by the cunning, ruthlessness, ability to manipulate others, to lie and conceal their personal feelings, but most of all, by their submission to the will of the 'Genius of all Time and Nations'.

By the time Glavny reached the pinnacle of power, he could no longer lay the claim to being a 'great leader'. He felt like a colt broken in by a superior rider. He could be as ruthless and domineering as he wished. He could even be capricious — but he could never be an untrammeled visionary. This is why he hated and secretly envied Mao so much.

But now the chance was his. Those soft-bodied Yanks, those capitalists who had never in their history had to cope with an invading power, were trying to challenge and intimidate him, the ruler of the long-suffering, the toughest, and now — potentially the wealthiest and strongest nation on Earth. He would show them! He would call their bluff.

Glavny pressed the button on his phone, and in response to a polite secretary's voice, shouted one word: "Vlas!" In a minute or two, the phone rang. Glavny switched on the loudspeaker to allow himself to pace the room while talking. Despite the pain he was feeling from his hemorrhoids, he needed somehow to release the energy that his anger about Mao had pushed into his bloodstream.

"How are the tests?"

"Brilliant, Glavny, simply brilliant. We can destroy ninety per cent of their land-based and fifty per cent of their submarine-based missiles in the first few minutes of war. Even if they master a concerted response after that, which is doubtful, our new laser interceptors will incapacitate eighty to ninety per cent of their oncoming missiles. At worst, we stand to lose a couple cities, maybe two or three million people in total. It's negligible."

"Look, Vlas, I want you to go ahead with the preparations. The second most important thing, as you realise of course, is the Bunker. Is it all set up?"

"The Bunker is totally secure, except for a direct 100-megaton-plus hit. We are putting the strongest laser defence shield around the Bunker, and inside there is a ten-year supply of food and water. I've even taken care of your favourite movies, 150 of them: Westerns, adventure, some soft porn that you like. And your favourite, *the Battle of Stalingrad*, of course."

"Good, good. Tell me, how is the anti-Socialin campaign going?"

"Last month, only 1,000 Party and government officials were executed. We seem to have reversed the trend."

"What is other news from around the country?"

"The increase in productivity has leveled off. Some experts consider this a reflection of civil disobedience on the part of the general population. Apparently, people aren't too happy about the purge against top officials that we are conducting. However, we still have sufficiently reliable cadres in the Party, Secret Police, and the Army to keep things under control. But it sure would be handy if the country could be united against an external enemy. You know, as you used to say yourself, that war is the greatest unifying force in times of peace."

"How many reliable people do you think we still have at the higher levels?"

"Oh, maybe a thousand, but I'm guessing. We have daily defections. Naturally, we have no reliable information as to how many of them may be taking Socialin on the sly. We can't screen them all at the Institute. We rely on confidential reports and clandestine observation. I'll be frank, Glavny, but for all I know, we may have executed many innocent people on false reports, while many of the clever ones are getting away with it. But we are doing the best we can, as usual. You know, when you cut down a forest, chips fly..."

"What else?"

"Nothing much. We've uncovered a small group of conspirators who decided to sabotage our project."

"Who are they?"

"Mostly small fry, a motley crew: rugged individuals, old Bolsheviks, some paramilitary, priests and monks, students, punks, ultranationalists, just the usual rabble."

"Put it on hold for now, we have more important things to think about right now," Glavny deliberated for a second, "and be ready for red alert. We've taken enough insults in the past sixty years. We'll call the capitalists' bluff this time."

"Whatever you say, Glavny."

In the quiet that filled the room after the loudspeakers fell silent, a loud crunch was heard. With great relish, Glavny wrenched the time lock off the top of his cigarette case. He didn't give a damn about the doctors and their warnings anymore. It was like the good old times during the war, or the purges, when you did not know from one day to the next whether you were going to be alive or dead. Who's worried about a stroke? One may as well enjoy what life has got to offer. To the very last.

Double Blind

Popov, the head of the team entrusted with the development of the new laser weapon system, was alone in his study when Richard brought in his weekly report. Popov greeted him and told him to wait a few minutes while he leafed through it.

Richard looked through a pile of periodicals on the table. Here they had everything — from *National Aeronautics* to the latest issues of *Scientific American* and *Jane's Catalogue*. But even here, in this highly classified establishment, staffed with the most trusted specialists, the relentless hand of the political censor made itself felt. Now and again, a page, usually an editorial with some political comment, would be missing. Sometimes, when the censors had been careless, the end of some important technical article would disappear along with it.

"Excellent, a highly original solution," Popov said, closing the folder Richard had brought. "But I can see one crucial flaw in your computer link-up between the lasers that will blind the enemy radars and at the same time make our offensive arsenal invisible."

"What's that?" Richard asked, looking rather innocent.

"You realise, of course, that after the decision to activate the system is made, the whole thing proceeds automatically and in a time scale so short that it defies human intervention. In other words, after you push the proverbial red button, the rest will be up to the computers."

"Yes, of course I realise that."

"Well, in your computer link-up system, there is this extremely vulnerable point in what you call the DDM section, where there is still a possibility of human intervention — you call it 'a manual error correction code' — being used on the system."

"Not if the computer is programmed to work in fully automatic mode," Richard countered. "I put that code in just for the test option."

"Yes, that is true. But this is about the only point where a human operator could influence the system unbeknownst to the High Command. Personally, I do not think you've built enough safeguards around this vulnerable point."

"I see what you mean," Richard said without the slightest emotion.

"Again," Popov picked up the folder and handed it over to Richard, looking him straight in the eye, "I don't think this is important enough to warrant a major revision at this stage, but if somebody else notices it, we might be in trouble."

"Who will notice it?" thought Richard. Certainly neither Vlas nor one of his overseers at the Ministry of Defence. The stuff they were working on was becoming so advanced and complex that, when it came to technical detail, he could swear that only he and Popov had any idea of what it was all about.

Richard had known about the flaw in his design. He was not sure whether he had consciously introduced it into the system after speaking to Swami or whether he was just following some inner impulse. It just came about that way. Even the system itself seemed to be devised in such a way as to require this minor flaw. To circumvent it would have required a re-draft of the entire system. It would have made it totally impervious to human error, but also bulky, inelegant, and difficult to test.

In fact, Richard did not expect even Popov to see it. But Popov, Richard had to admit, was a smart cookie. At first, he barely followed Richard's train of thought and came up with some pretty nonsensical suggestions that Richard simply ignored. But lately he was becoming much more involved and quick to latch onto Richard's ideas.

"You know," Popov changed his tone, indicating that the formal part of their meeting was over, "I've been getting a little philosophical lately about the work we do here."

"Yes," Richard answered guardedly, "I don't think one can avoid becoming a little philosophical about the nature of our work."

"At times," Popov continued, "I'll tell you as a scientist to a scientist, the entire thing strikes me as being a bit crazy. We are playing with consequences we barely understand, let alone predict. And what for?"

"Similar thoughts have occasionally occurred to me, too," Richard nodded in agreement.

"You see, we work on the presumption that the system might one day be used, and yet we know that if it were used, it would nullify all of the reasons for it being there in the first place. I mean for being there as a defensive system."

"I think there may be a bit of doublethink involved here," consented Richard. "While the system isn't operative, it is effective, and we can think of it in terms like 'deterrence' or 'balance of fear'. But if anyone decides to use it, we become involved in a sort of collective insanity that leads to mutual destruction perhaps of a large proportion of the world population and of the earth's ecosystems. Think of it, it would be crazy to even press the button in retaliation, except as an act of blind revenge, which would be directed mostly against the innocent civilian population on the other side. It's a crazy thing to do when you know that you are already practically dead yourself."

Richard stopped, feeling that he may have gone too far.

Popov suddenly put on a cheerful smile and said, "I hope — don't we all? — that nobody will ever push the button. To make the final insanity impossible, unfortunately, we must continue working on insane assumptions — there is another piece of doublethink for you."

Popov rose and indicated to Richard that the discussion was over.

"But what about that design flaw?" queried Richard. "Do you want me to correct it?"

"Not now. Frankly, I don't think it is important enough. We'll probably be updating the whole system in a few months, so we could do it then. It would be a pity to change it now — technically, it looks so... so... perfect." Snowden knew that Popov was under tremendous pressure from Glavny to present the results fast.

Richard moved towards the door.

"Tell me," Popov delayed him for another moment. "Did you really find that your thinking improved after you took that pill and started meditating at the same time?"

"Undoubtedly," Richard was adamant. "It took me two weeks to solve the problem that had tormented me for years. And there are other things..."

"I understand," Popov replied, looking him straight in the eye and shaking hands with him in a manner that made Richard wonder whether he too had joined the band of Socialin takers. "I'll see you in a week's time."

The Unthinkable Happens

A Report to the President. Top Secret

Our sources inform us that in the past few weeks and especially after your secret memorandum to the Soviet leadership on the Sino-Soviet question, some large-scale military preparations are being made by the Soviets. It appears that they are completely unaware of our newly acquired first-strike capability and are trying to resort to their traditional bluff tactics. We advise you and the State Department to adopt an even firmer attitude over the Sino-Soviet question. The Soviet demands for reduction of our troops in Western Europe and for closure of Radio Liberty and Radio Free Europe, in exchange for their neutrality in the Middle East conflict, should also be rejected. Now, as never before, we are in a position to stand up to the Soviets and call their bluff. Purely as a matter of precaution, we recommend placing our strategic forces around the world on red alert.

Signed: The Director, Central Intelligence Agency.

The lift slid noiselessly down to Level A of the Bunker. It carried Glavny and his entourage — Vlas, two bodyguards, and a bristle of soldiers, one of them carefully carrying a small suitcase in his hand. They were 1,000 feet underground. Only forty-five seconds had gone by since they had left Glavny's study. Already, they would have been out of reach of any but the most direct and powerful nuclear blasts.

A small bullet-shaped carriage, which looked more like a spacecraft than a train, stood at the door of the lift. They entered it, and as soon as the door shut, it sped downwards into another concrete and lead-encased pit that took them to Level B. Glavny hated this part of the journey most of all. It was the sensation of free-fall that he particularly disliked. It was explained to him that the air cushion at the bottom of the pit would stop the carriage smoothly, and that there was no way it could malfunction, since there were no cables or electrical circuits that could break down. Glavny had repeated this journey a number of times during trial alerts, but he had never got used to it. Every time they went down into the seemingly endless fall, he felt out of control. He hated to rely on physical laws, even when they were on his side.

They walked briskly into the Level B enclosure. It resembled not so much a conventional bomb shelter as a large underground apartment building with kitchens, bathrooms, and dining rooms filled with metal tables lined up in perfect rows. There was a small movie theatre and a table tennis room.

It was not comfortable or pleasing to the eye — everything was subordinated to the demands of space, economy, and safety — but it could not be called Spartan either. Along light green and blue metal walls there were numerous signs indicating access to supply chutes: "Water", "Dry Foods", "Liquid Foods", "Disposable Clothing", "Gas Masks", "Medicines."

Soon, this underground apartment house would be filled with 300-odd members of the Party, government and military elite, accompanied by their immediate families. Glavny had personally approved the list the evening before, having revised it a few times. To gain a place on this list, known among the staffers as the "Red Ark", was the most coveted privilege in the Soviet hierarchy. For years now, Glavny had used it as the ultimate weapon in his struggle to ensure subordination and to keep the power struggle under control. The threat of being struck off the list brought even the toughest opponents to heel. The promise to be put on it made the laziest apparatchik strive for excellence. Occasionally, informing some recalcitrant member of the Politburo that he could not, for example, take his son or daughter with him could exert additional pressure.

At turbulent times — as when Pavlovich and his associates were plotting to oust Glavny, saying that his policy of *detente* with the Americans had failed, and when another palace coup seemed imminent — the list was subject to inflationary pressures. Even though the Bunker could accommodate only about 100 families, 300 people in total, Glavny had given assurances to as many as 400 that they were, "On the Ark." Since he was the only one who had access to the final list till the last moment, nobody could check on him. And the privileged carried their secret with the faint smugness of a chosen race. Just a mysterious smile, a firmer gait, greater impatience in dealing with inferiors, and tougher views on international politics.

Finally, a massive door at the end of the corridor swung open to the keying of a code by Vlas. They were in the innermost part of the Bunker, Level C, reserved for Glavny, his closest associates, and his personal bodyguard. It was also a War Room. There were screens and maps on the wall. Level C had its own supply of food, water, and electricity.

As they entered the room, one of the bodyguards put down a basket he was carrying and opened the lid. A small black poodle jumped out. It was Glavny's pet, 'Pushok' ('Fluffy'). Glavny could not contemplate leaving him behind, and anyway, his psychiatrist had told him that the dog's company was good for him in times of crisis, as it provided him with reassurance, warmth, and love. It was not his fault that ever since he became 'Glavny' he could no longer find these qualities in his friends, and not even among his close family circle. Everyone tried to use him and his power to promote their own interests.

There was no time to be lost. The General opened the case he had been carrying. It turned out to be a portable computer, combined with an electronic transmitting device. It was the proverbial 'red bag' that was always close to Glavny wherever he went, and which was necessary to begin the complicated set of operations necessary to begin World War III.

The screens in the room jumped to life. The voice of the operator somewhere on Level B announced that most of the people to whom notice could be given in time were already in the Bunker. Only five families were still missing.

"To hell with them," hissed Vlas. "We can't afford to lose any more time! Tell them to deactivate the Level A entrance."

Glavny nodded in agreement. One of the officers pressed a button on the panel. "The Tyumen missile complex is ready," he announced.

"And what is the enemy's position?" asked Glavny.

"Still on red alert, but no unexpected movements or developments in the last half hour."

"I'm sure they're still regarding this as a training alert," remarked Vlas.

"We'll show them that at last we mean business," said Glavny with a mean smirk, motioning to Vlas to bring the case to him.

It had no single button. Actually, it had to be programmed by a combination of numbers that was picked up by a specially assigned officer from a table each day. After that a second person — in this case, Vlas — had to punch a few more numbers to verify the order. This was to safeguard against Glavny's sudden insanity or the unlikely case of someone forcing Glavny to start a war. Glavny could still start it himself but, unless backed up by a second person who knew a different code, he would have to communicate his decision directly to the Chief of Staff, who could then manually overrule the safeguard.

Glavny's hand hovered over the keyboard. The room fell silent. There was only the mute blinking of the screens and the soft whimpering of Pushok, who was trying to get his master's attention by rubbing against his leg. Glavny noticed that Vlas' hands, still grasping the outside of the red case, were trembling slightly.

"You damn beast." Glavny, who was usually gentle with his dog, shoved Pushok away. "Don't bother me now."

Deliberately, as if trying not to make a mistake, he punched in a series of numbers on the keyboard. Everyone in the room watched his movements with intense concentration. The unthinkable was happening. Vlas forgot what he had to do after Glavny had finished.

"Come on, wake up." Glavny's voice brought him back to reality. "Have you forgotten your code?"

"No, no, I remember it," mumbled Vlas. He walked around to face the keyboard and, as if in a dream, punched in another six-digit combination.

The war was on! No human intervention could stop now the pitiless Doomsday Machine from grinding to its conclusion. Glavny had to use his cigarette lighter twice to get a light.

In his mind's eye, Glavny saw the picture they had so often rehearsed during the war games. Their new laser system was disabling enemy radars on the land, in the air, and aboard spy satellites. The enemy guidance systems were being disrupted by a combination of electronic and laser interference. And simultaneously, dozens of MIRV rockets — dozens were all that was needed to cripple the enemy without producing impermissible levels of fallout throughout the globe — were on their way to their targets.

New York, the City of the Yellow Devil, as one Russian writer had called it, perished in one blinding flash. In Washington, Los Angeles, Chicago, all around the country, underground silos exploded while Russian nuclear killer submarines struck with deadly precision. Even if some of the American submarines were able to launch their rockets, chances were that most of them would be disabled by the new Soviet anti-ballistic missile laser defence system.

Glavny's fists clenched until his knuckles became white. Yes, this was the moment he had been waiting for all his life. Skyscrapers crumbling to the ground like children's toys, huge cars hurled into the air and pulverised into dust together with their occupants. Panic, incomprehension, and then, swift death. To Glavny, this meant more than physical destruction. It was the destruction of a symbol, a way of life that was eternally threatening to people like him. This way of life was supposed to have perished around the middle of the 20th century, torn by internal contradictions, strikes, violence, and an inept foreign policy.

But it refused to go away. Despite the incessant talk of economic collapse, it still managed to maintain an economy which was far stronger than that of its Communist rival. Despite the continuing threat of an internal rift, it produced virtually no defections from the capitalist camp to the socialist, while literally thousands — scientists, ballet dancers, writers, all sorts of people — run the other way.

Now, everything will be different. The capitalist world that refused to conform to Marxist predictions will be purified by something it could not resist — fire, death. The way for the glorious triumph of the proletariat, led by Glavny's Party, by Glavny himself, will be opened across the globe. Involuntarily, Glavny raised himself from his chair, as if preparing to review a parade in the Red Square, in which not only his countrymen, but also delegations from all over the world would march in lock step, expressing gratitude and devotion to the Great Leader who had restored peace and harmony to this strife-torn planet.

There was confusion in the room. The lights on the screens and panels blinked once or twice and then went off. Only the emergency lights on the ceiling stayed on. Sensing anxiety and agitation in the room, Pushok whimpered softly. Glavny looked at Vlas, who was holding tightly to the edge of the table, as if expecting a strong jolt. They both knew that something, somewhere, had gone terribly wrong.

Message to America

The traffic light changed to red and the driver gently eased his car to a stop. To the right, people were eating lunch in the park. A group of boys played soccer in the middle of the field. A young girl ran across the street in front of a slow moving car, playfully pushing against the hood, and peeking inside mischievously.

The driver looked at her admiringly, and turning to his passenger, said something that made him laugh. A car behind honked briefly, as the light had already changed. Everywhere, crowds of lunchtime shoppers were swarming around the city, aware only of July's heat and the bustling movement of people and cars. The car drove up to the side entrance in the Kremlin wall.

An officer examined their passes. "Mr Snowden, Colonel Lavrov, please proceed to the Third Floor, Room 1. Comrade Popov is expecting you."

Richard noticed that the officer was not wearing the standard uniform of the Kremlin guard with epaulettes, but an Air Force outfit.

They went up to the third floor, showing their passes at two more checkpoints. Another Air Force officer led them to the door at the end of the corridor. Underneath the brass plaque with heavily embossed words, "First Secretary", hung a makeshift paper sign, saying simply, "Commander-in-Chief, Comrade Popov."

Motioned by the officer, they entered the room. Richard looked around. There were about twenty people in the room, most of them in military uniform. Richard knew Popov and recognized a few other Ministry of Defence personnel. There were also a number of high-ranking officers from the Navy and the Rocket Corps.

Conversation ceased and all eyes focused on Richard and Lavrov. Popov rose from his chair and announced,

"Comrades, this is our friend and colleague, Richard Snowden, about whom I told you earlier. Without his expert assistance, we would not have been able to prevent the nuclear catastrophe that might have taken place this morning."

Popov continued. "He incorporated a flaw into the offensive system, which made it possible for us, who did not want the atomic nightmare to become a reality, to intervene at the crucial moment, and to prevent the outbreak of war.

"Mr Snowden, as a sign of special gratitude and recognition of your services, you will have the privilege of being the first person to speak on the Red Line to your President in Washington. We have an important message to convey to him and," Popov smiled broadly, "we would be grateful if it was conveyed in fluent English. You see, the First Secretary's official interpreter is slightly indisposed."

He handed Richard a piece of paper, lifted the telephone receiver, and said a few words to the operator. There was a loud click on the line and a voice that was familiar to Richard from radio broadcasts was heard on the other end.

"This is the President of the United States."

"Mr President," Richard began to read the message, hardly able to concentrate on its meaning, "on behalf of the newly-formed Russian government, I would like to inform you that there is absolutely no threat of nuclear attack from our side. We have just carried out a revolution, a peaceful revolution, in our country. Temporarily, all power is in the hands of a Special Committee, comprising representatives of the Armed Forces and some civilian leaders. However, as soon as the situation stabilizes we will conduct the first democratic election ever held in this country. We hope that we can rely on your cooperation, goodwill, and non-interference in our internal affairs during the transition period."

"If this is not some sort of a giant hoax, I assure you that you will have my fullest cooperation," the voice boomed at the other end of the line.

Richard related the answer to Popov, who translated it into Russian. There was a burst of applause. Popov took over the phone and said, in his heavily accented English, "My name is Andrei Popov and I have been nominated as Head of Special Committee and as Commander-in-Chief of the military forces. I will keep you informed about the developments in our country. We appreciate your offer of cooperation and non-interference."

Popov thanked Richard for his help and resumed the conference with his advisers. Richard left the room, accompanied by Colonel Lavrov.

"I'm still not too sure if even I can fully understand what happened this morning," the Colonel said, "but I guess I can tell you now. Our government — our former government, I should say — made an attempt to begin a global war at five a.m. this morning. Lately, there had been a lot of opposition to the leadership among high government, military, and Party officials. Too many people were taking Socialin secretly, as well as practicing meditation, and Vlas and his henchmen executed too many innocent victims. It was a game of roulette — a true Russian roulette, you might say. One morning you were fine and the next you were gone. So, when it became apparent that the leadership was seriously considering launching a war, the opposition united under the leadership of Comrade Popov. Fortunately, through your work you provided him with the means of preventing the launching of the missiles."

Richard listened attentively, hardly believing his ears.

"Then we cut off all communications between the Bunker and the outside world. For all they knew down there, we could all have been wiped out by the retaliatory strike of the enemy. They must be preparing now to sit it out for the next few months or — even years, until the radioactivity on the surface reaches a safe level."

"And what are you going to do — just let them stay there?"

"No, our technicians are working on possible ways of bugging the closed-circuit T.V. in the Bunker. We'll see what we can do then. We must be prepared to somehow deal with them after we have held our first democratic elections. And that might take some time. After that, they may be tried for as war criminals in the Hague, for attempting genocide on a global scale, a crime for which there are no legal precedents.

"And what's going to happen to me?" he ventured.

"Comrade Popov has told me that you will be allowed to leave the country and go wherever you wish, when things calm down a little. At the moment, all international traffic in and out of Moscow airport has been temporarily suspended."

Four days later, the phone rang in Richard's room. "This is Colonel Lavrov speaking. Please come down to the Kremlin immediately. I have already given orders to your bodyguard and the driver."

Richard could only guess the reason for this sudden call. He had kept in touch with the outside world by listening to the radio and reading papers. In the absence of Glavny and his most ardent supporters, the transfer of power in the country seemed to have gone on relatively smoothly.

Local authorities had, even before the takeover, assumed much greater responsibility over the affairs of the country. They were now preparing to conduct the first democratic elections in Russian history. This was not an easy task. People had to be convinced that they could actually nominate candidates who were not the appointees of the Party, and that they could vote against other people's candidates.

As soon as they entered the Kremlin compound, Richard guessed that some sort of emergency operation was afoot. There were huge army trucks rigged with complicated electronic gear and rescue teams equipped to deal with radiation hazards.

In the corridor, Richard accidentally bumped into a Russian priest with a triangular beard walking along a young student. "Father Timofei," the young man was gesticulating, talking with excitement, "Revolution can be good for the Soul; we need to help the good to fight the evil in the world." The couple disappeared down the long corridor, still gesticulating wildly.

Richard and his escort were taken to a basement room in one of the ancillary buildings close to the Kremlin wall. There were military personnel everywhere. Thick cables were lying on the floor of the corridor leading to the trucks above on the ground.

Popov greeted them briefly as they walked into a room which looked like the control room of a large power station. Along the walls, there were numerous television screens and control panels. Popov took Richard to the side, out of the way of people who were busily carrying more equipment in, shouting instructions and swearing.

"It seems we might be able to peek into the Level C Bunker in a few minutes," said Popov. "As you can imagine, this is an extremely complicated operation. They tried to make sure that what we are doing now could not be done — unless, of course, one has the expertise of those very specialists who installed the gear in the first place." He looked at the television screens on the wall, just above eye level. "Aha, look there... something is happening."

A blurry image on the screen was taking shape and becoming clearer. Dark shadows of people were gradually beginning to appear, although it was still impossible to recognize who they were.

"Look," somebody shouted. "There is one of the display maps on the west wall of the Bunker. I know it, I wired it myself."

"Tell them to try and see if they can lower the camera," Popov commanded. A few more minutes passed in anxious expectation.

"Look," another voice shouted. "See those marks on the wall — they're bullet holes."

"No," someone else suggested, "they're control buttons."

"No, they're not; there are no control buttons on the west wall."

"Oh, my God," somebody gasped. The whispers and noise in the room subsided. The camera's eye had focused on the figure of a man in military uniform, lying prostrate on the floor. Half the man's skull appeared blown off as if by some terrific explosion.

The camera continued its journey through the room. There was another figure, its limbs hanging limply from the chair.

"He's got a gun in his hand," noted the operator.

"I recognize him," Popov said softly. "It's Vlas. And there's... Glavny."

The camera focused on a slumped figure pushed against the wall as if by some invisible force. There was a large, dark puddle on the floor around him. Nobody said a word, as if even now the slumped figure against the wall could rise up and unleash its anger upon the spectators.

"And what's that?" Somebody finally broke the silence. "There is someone alive."

They saw a dark figure standing in the middle of the room, automatic gun at the ready.

"But that's Saffron, Glavny's chief bodyguard!"

There was a period of silence as the people digested what they saw.

"Has he gone crazy?" someone suggested.

"Was there some sort of fight? Is there anyone alive at Level C?"

"The technicians have intercepted the whimpering of a dog in the Bunker at Level C."

"I am sure he will not be regarded as an accomplice..." Colonel Lavrov joked.

"I sure hope not," Richard smiled back.

"What happened to the people in Level B? Can we get a camera to work in there?"

"How long do you think it will take us to break into the Bunker?" Popov asked a man in white overalls and a crash helmet, interrupting a barrage of questions in the room.

"We must at least get the women and children out of there. And we have to act fast."

"Maybe days, but hopefully, hours," the man replied. "You appreciate that we can't blow the entrance with ordinary explosives; it's been made to withstand a direct atomic blast. And at Level C the entrance can be opened from the inside only."

Bewildered and shocked by what he had just witnessed, Richard walked slowly out of the room, led by Colonel Lavrov. They went out to the car with a driver waiting outside. The Kremlin, with its majestic golden cupolas of domed churches piercing the sky, seemed like a floating island from some fairy tale. Lavrov shook Richard's hand and said warmly, "Goodbye. They will reopen the Sheremetyevo International Airport in a few hours."

Richard nodded.

"You know," the Colonel hesitated momentarily before uttering his parting remark, "all these years I thought I was serving a sane government. Now, I'm no longer sure."

"That was the illusion I was living under as well in my country," Richard responded.

"But do you know," Richard asked, "what finally happened to Swami?"

"Oh, he left for India. I spoke to him before he left. He said that he was going to continue his work to bring world peace. Good luck to the old fellow. After what we have just seen, I am not sure that we can ever overcome man's crazy behavior."

"What else did Swami say?"

"He spoke against the continued use of Socialin. He said it had served its purpose — it gave us the temporary breathing space we needed. People should be allowed to go their own way. And he also added that he is hoping that you can join him in India one day.

"I just hope," Lavrov smiled, "that your Swami will not go batty, like some of these gurus do, and start some silly cult, like teaching people to fly or something…"

"I sure hope so," Richard replied. "But you never know…"

Homeward

The car left and Richard turned to wave to Colonel Lavrov, a tall figure standing immobile in the middle of the driveway, his hand raised in the habitual military salute.

The Lufthansa flight to New York via Vienna was forty-five minutes late because of a severe thunderstorm raging over Moscow.

In the entrance hall, Richard saw Dr Larchuk, madly waving at him.

Richard thought how fortunate it was that Dr Larchuk had come to see him off and that there was someone to talk to during the delay. They went to the cafeteria and ordered snacks.

Dr Larchuk was speaking about the research he was doing, about his separation from his wife after he had quit his job with the government. "She wants me to come back now, but I'm not sure if I ever will. And you," Dr Larchuk looked at Richard quizzically. "Aren't you afraid to go back home, I mean to the US?"

Richard looked at him closely. "Oh, you mean because I've divulged military secrets and was, although under duress, working for a foreign government?"

"Yes, I suppose that's the gist of it."

"Well, I could move to a neutral country but, apparently, the new Russian government made a request on my behalf to the Americans and, as far as I've been told, all is forgiven.

"I am sure they will give me a very close debriefing but, hopefully, not as severe as the one I have gotten in the hands of the KGB," Richard smiled, his smile looking a little forced.

"You know, they may suspect I have become a triple agent."

"A *triple* agent?" Dr Larchuk mused.

"Yes, working for Russia, for the US — after all who put a false code into the launch program? — and maybe for 'world peace', together with Swami."

"I meant it as a bit of a joke, of course," he hastened to add, not wishing to sound corny.

"But do you trust the US government? Don't you think that there are people like Vlas and Glavny also who may not be too happy with the way things have worked out?"

"Oh, sure," said Richard. "But I believe in a democratic society we have ways of influencing our leaders which need not be quite as dramatic as yours."

"You know," Dr Larchuk looked at Richard intently, "I am not so sure your democracy is much better than ours when it comes to governments and wars..."

"If I were you, I would seriously consider Swami's invitation to come and work with him in India. You'll be a lot safer that way. Together, you can develop natural alternatives to Socialin. You can let the families of the people who were killed by the KGB on that plane over the Bermuda Triangle know what really happened to their loved ones. The American media is bound to distort and sensationalize the story. You could write a book about it and... maybe even make a mint from it. Isn't this how the capitalist society works?"

Richard listened without making any comments. He will have time to think about the future and maybe even change his flight in Vienna and go to a safe location.

"You know, about the 'world peace' you mentioned..." Dr Larchuk paused, listening to the announcement over the loudspeaker saying that flights would be resumed in half an hour. "Until very recently, I used to hold pretty pessimistic views about mankind's future."

"And now you have changed your mind?"

"Look," Dr Larchuk's voice was becoming loud and passionate. "When, millions of years ago, we fell out of the trees onto the arid savanna, we had to kill and scavenge our way out of extinction. We learned to kill in packs like wolves, and we just couldn't stop killing, even when the spear was replaced by the atomic bomb. But we also retained, through all the hardships, something like a divine spark in us."

Richard sat quietly.

"So you think the divine spark is still alive in us and can even win over the war habit?" he asked, looking at Dr Larchuk intently.

"I was reading in yesterday morning's *The New York Times* that even in America, sixty per cent of the population is already doing the American brand of meditation," said Richard. "At first, it spread there just like it did here; it increased productivity and boosted military capacity. But then it just took off by itself. People must have longed for something like that, and when it came, there was no turning back. Humans will never cease looking for lost paradise."

"Passengers traveling to Vienna aboard Lufthansa Flight 784 should now proceed to the boarding area," came the announcement.

Richard rose. "Thanks for coming to see me off. I will always remember your country — after all, I nearly died and was reborn here, and even... fell in love... briefly."

"Speaking of love," Dr Larchuk's eyes twinkled, "I nearly forgot. Here is a little present for you from... your admirer. She couldn't come to see you off — busy at work — she has joined the Bunker rescue team...." He took a slim, hard cover volume from his briefcase and handed it to Richard.

Richard opened the volume. It was a collection of poems by the Russian poet Alexander Pushkin, translated into English. He noticed a bookmark and opened the page. A pencil line ran along the margin of a verse.

It's time, my friend, it's time! My heart craves quietude.
Oh, fleeting days, nay, hours ...
Each ticking off a portion of one's life. Yes, you and I –
Expect to live forever. But Death arrives by stealth.
Life is a vale of tears but peace and joy are free.
I dreamed for long to find such peace;
I, tired slave of life, dreamed of escaping
To a refuge, far away, of toil and pure delights.

He felt a sudden pang of emotion. She remembered him, made a connection though this cryptic verse. What did she mean by 'a refuge, far away'? Surely, she is not hinting to him that she might join him in some neutral country? Oh, the mind of a woman is hard to read, but the mind of a spy-woman is well-nigh impossible to know... Will she still work as a spy for the new Russia? Somehow he doubted it. She would probably like to leave her past behind... She, like him, paid her dues and could consider herself no longer in bondage.

Dr Larchuk touched him on the shoulder. "It's time to go; you'll miss your plane. And you know..." he hesitated briefly. "The plane stops for refueling in Vienna and you can catch a connecting flight to India then. And, by the way... I am not supposed to tell you this, but I have heard that Anna asked for a transfer to the Ministry of Foreign Affairs and is hoping to get a posting in the Russian embassy in New Delhi."

Richard smiled appreciatively, struck by Dr Larchuk's attention. They shook hands.

"Good luck, *droog**."

The air outside the terminal was filled with the spring freshness that follows a heavy thunderstorm.

---

* "Friend" in Russian.

Appendix A

Scientists win Nobel Prize for medicine for research into psychedelically catalyzed meditation (PCM) to combat drug and alcohol addiction, improve productivity and general well-being

I want to see such a headline in five years' time. Not in 20 years or 50 years. I have been following research into this topic for over 40 years. I have written **Project Nirvana**. I have known some of the leading scientists in the field. I mourn the decades lost after Nixon declared his "war on drugs" to ward off his fear of losing a whole generation to the anti-Vietnam war movement.

Decades lost: Now, billions of dollars and untold human losses later (to imprisonment, violence, addiction, trauma and damage to whole communities), the research is still being hampered by government controls, resistance from the Big Pharma and the medical research establishment. A researcher may still waste months to get his/her research approval, and tens of thousands of dollars to get medicines that were freely available in the 50s and 60s at virtually no cost.

It's the economy, stupid. We need to be bolder. We do not need to prove again and again that psilocybin is safer and more effective for treatment of anxiety and PTSD than any known prescription drug, or that MDMA is useful for family therapy. What we do need to show is that psychedelic medicines can improve general well-being and health, enhance productivity and enjoyment of life, and replace damaging, expensive, and ineffective drugs. It seems that what may finally sway our governments will be economics. We simply will not be able to afford to **lock up our young in prisons** for mere possession of marijuana. And we will need our **old folks to work**

productively well into their pension years.

New paradigm: save money, reach more people. We need to be both bold AND pragmatic, cheap and effective. In addition to testing new medicines on some morbidly sick or dying people, or, at the other extreme, on "advanced" meditators to see the effects that a particular plant extract will have on them, we need to test healthy people with PCM to see the effect on their general health, well-being, and productivity. Earlier studies proved the existence of "the relaxation response" (thus making meditation respectable), and confirmed morphological changes which meditation and relaxation produced in patients' cardiovascular systems.

Right now we can use **simple and inexpensive tools** to show what kind of difference PCM can make. For example, we can use heart rate variability (**HRV**), which is being increasingly used by our elite athletes, to monitor the improvement of a subject's general health and fitness. HRV is perhaps the most sensitive measure of fitness as manifested by the subtle balance between alternating periods of rest and activity in the autonomous nervous system, often damaged by stress. There are a number of simple and inexpensive gadgets available to anyone right now to monitor HRV in real time.

Simple test for brain integration: At the other end of the scale, we could use tests developed by the late Dr Herbert Spiegel, a Columbia University psychiatrist, who introduced the term "**neural trance.**"[1] These tests (known as **HIP** or "hypnotic induction profile") require no expensive equipment. They measure the level of intactness of the CNS and the coherence and "flow" of neural traffic between different brain areas, indicating the degree of stress-free functioning. In the same way in which HRV measures physical health, HIP could be used as a powerful indicator of psychological health.

Later on: When such inexpensive and simple tests prove

---

1 http://iiceh.com/pdf/neutraltrance.pdf

the desirable health effects of PCM for the general population, we can apply more advanced medical technologies, such as non-invasive deep brain imaging and stimulation, fMRI, etc., to further substantiate the results.

Researchers self-experiment: Such research will no doubt bring improvements in protocols and tools. We can gradually reduce doses of psychedelics; we can combine such micro-doses with new memory and brain enhancement substances until the psychedelic catalyst can be withdrawn completely or spaced as widely as desired. We can provide set-and-settings improvements that will only come when researchers themselves are able to use their own experimentation with PCM to increase their perception of age-old truths and to interrogate traditional/shamanistic guides more fruitfully.

Four Horsemen of the epidemiological Apocalypse: With humanity increasingly confronting its most testing challenges, we will be able to relate such research more closely to advances in genetics, biology, and evolutionary psychology. We can then define and measure the individual's Transcendence Quotient or TQ - the ability to experience altered states of consciousness and integrate them, its genetic and personality basis, and adjust our regimens accordingly. It may be too early to dream of integrating bionics and genetic enhancements into this quest but such may be our horizons sooner than we think.

The health of any nation is crucial to its progress. In Australia, our underfunded and overstretched traditional medicine is losing its ground to the Four Horsemen of the modern epidemiological Apocalypse: **Stress, Addiction, Obesity, and Depression.** Medicine is pointlessly tilling the ground that is being flattened by the horses' hooves. With our ageing population, the burden on the health system will soon become simply unbearable.

I have no doubt that countries that make intelligent use of psychedelics and meditation will prosper and advance more than others.

Appendix B

Are Drugs Experimenting with Humans?

Disclaimer: The article was written during the height of the "war on drugs." The newspaper lawyers and editors went over every word so that nothing could be construed as encouraging people to take drugs. It was a miracle it got published at all!

Little did I know that this article was going to be prophetic and that I could still sign my name under it some 20 years later.

The emotions were (and are) so high that even now people misconstrue things, even after reading the article.

So, let me make this clear:

1) I called for "drug use" to be STUDIED as a subject at high school, maybe as part of life sciences, i.e. as an "Introduction to Ethnobotany."

2) I came out against outright legalization of all drugs without proper training and preparation.

To give anyone *carte blanche* for drug use would be similar to allowing anyone to drive a car without a licence and proper training, road rules, traffic cops, etc.

3) For informed adults, psychedelic medicines and plants may be used only as CATALYSTS for meditation under proper supervision and training, to be reduced to micro-doses and discontinued as soon as possible in favor of pure meditation.

The original illustration and article begin on the next page.

Are Drugs Experimenting with Humans?

PYOTR PATRUSHEV considers some radical new thinking about drug addiction in the world's worst-affected nation.

Education is key. I believe that the only long-term way to win the drug war is to introduce drug use into the classroom as a legitimate subject starting with, say, Grade 9.

I am not speaking out of total ignorance, and only partly tongue-in-cheek. For, during my recent trip to the US, I have taken an active part in the drug war, in the role, alas, of a civilian casualty.

I was walking along Sutter Street in San Francisco, in broad daylight, close to the usually safe Japantown. A gang of black youths were walking in the opposite direction. They were well-fed and dressed in smart track suits and casual clothes — not your usual derelict types who would push the streetwise button of a visitor.

I made eye contact with one of them, as he was trying to attract my attention by wild gesticulation. What happened next was a blur of movement and pain. I was kicked in the stomach and punched in the eye. As I fell to the ground, I saw the youths run.

They were not interested in my money. They were not muggers. They were high, possibly on crack. They were engaging in a self-designed, juvenile "hit-a-white-and-get-away-with-it" initiation ritual. I just happened to be the bloke with the whitest skin on the block.

I am not saying that the drug problem is in any way a racial problem. Heavy use of drugs by blacks is only one of its many facets. It is true that in the Highland Hospital in Oakland, in the San Francisco Bay Area, 45 per cent of all randomly tested, mostly black, patients showed crack metabolites in their blood.

It is also true that in New York, 73 percent of arrested women, again mostly black, tested positive for cocaine. Equally true, drug use in perhaps less eye-catching fashion, affects all races and ill strata of the community in the US as it does elsewhere.

What I found out through this bitter personal experience is that the drug war, unleashed initially by the ebulliently optimistic if hare-brained Nixon, has left one with no place to hide.

Thinking of the staid Berkeley City Council's suggestion to introduce snifter dogs into the streets and homes of this university town, I appreciated the relative safety of Australia. And I wondered how long it would last.

Could we learn something from the American experience? This year, the US Government earmarked a staggering $US8 billion ($A10.25 billion) for drug war. This sounds like a lot of money, until we learn that the illicit drug trade will net the equivalent of the entire Federal Budget deficit in the same year — a cool $US150 billion.

Yet, only a small percentage — 5 to 7 percent — of heroin and cocaine traffic crossing the border will be intercepted. These days it costs $US2 million to catch and jail a single drug smuggler, plus around $US18.000 a year to keep him in custody for 10 to 20 years. As one prominent American columnist had suggested, it would be cheaper — as well as much easier, although not as glamorous — to BUY smugglers off the street at $US2 million a shot and to allow them a comfortable retirement in Miami.

But even if the law enforcement agencies significantly cut the cocaine and heroin supply routes — which is unlikely — they will not snuff the demand. Just as the barons of the Medellin cartel in Bogota seem to be beating a temporary retreat, Asian and other cartels are coming on to the market with a new smokable form of amphetamine (called "ice"), which is far more addictive and easier to smuggle and manufacture locally than cocaine-derived crack.

We can only control it. A leading US psychopharmacologist and drug expert, Dr Ronald Siegel of UCLA, joined recently the growing band of specialists who say we cannot stop the drug use, only learn to control it. He calls the use of plant-derived psychoactive substances (of which alcohol is an example) "the fourth natural drive" and proves that it is as widespread in the animal kingdom as it is in the human and had been throughout evolution.

He goes as far as to suggest that we may need to design better and safer psychoactive drugs and ways of using them rather than trying simply to prohibit their use.

The major problem with the current generation of drugs, experts such as Ron Siegel argue, is their illegality, their incredible potency (itself a product of science wreaking its belated revenge on man's presumptuous brain), and the abysmal ignorance of both the users and the controllers of use about the evolutionary nature and purpose of drug experience.

Drugs are now recognized as problem number one both in the US and in Australia, ahead of even such terrors as crime and inflation, and far ahead of war. Yet our response to this problem has been, it seems, somewhat myopic.

The proposed legalization of drugs, which is regarded by some as enlightened, only perpetuates the problem of ignorant and health-damaging abuse, sacrificing large portions of the population, mostly young, for the relative peace of the rest.

An old Sufi tale says: "You can only use what you have learnt to use." It advises to train the genie to obey your commands before you let him out of the bottle.

An ethnobotanical expert in the US has suggested that human culture is in fact shaped by the historical interaction of people and plants, including psychoactive plants. **Man, he said, might be just an experiment by plants, and, moreover, one that is a cause for grave concern to the rest of the biosphere.**

This is less whimsical than it sounds when we recall that such major social upheavals as slavery and opium wars were precipitated by man's uncontrollable addiction to white sugar, tea, and, finally, the extract of a poppy plant.

Coca-dollars are now a major political factor in the financial world. Just to think what a tobacco plant has done to humanity's health and finances boggles one's mind.

Other experts tell us that if you dig at the root of all modern religions you will find a plant-derived ritual. Plants were used for vision quests and initiations, thereby forging the link between the established cultural tradition and the aspirations of the young generation.

Can we put a claim to be at least as intelligent as plants, so that we can reverse the direction of our war on drugs — which is actually an unmitigated retreat — and take some charge of the experiment being supposedly carried out by intelligent plants on our incumbent civilization?

Can we see in 25 years' time (or is it 10, or five?) school kits with homeopathic or superdiluted extracts of psychoactive plants from all over the world being available for experimentation, together with detailed description of plant action and their ritual use?

Can we see our teachers of psychology finally being able to explain and possibly guide not just the behavior of rats in a maze, but the craving Gutenberg felt for fermented grapes whose juice made him see an image of the printing press for the first time, thus initiating one of the most significant revolutions in human history?

Can we see field trips to the Amazonian jungle and the forests of Siberia or North Queensland (were there still such in existence) to discover the ethnobotanical lore and traditions, which have guided intelligent use of psychoactive plans throughout millennia?

Or shall we simply buy more radars and high-speed chase boats and give police robotized battering-rams to break reinforced doors of crack or "ice" — or whatever — dens?

We have come a long way from the drug paranoia of the 50s to the rebellious euphoria of the 60s to the sober pragmatism of the late-80s. We have learnt that drug epidemics, as well as interest rates surges and recessions, come in waves whose laws seem, at this stage, more familiar to plants than to our human planners. **Perhaps the time has come to study them as a legitimate subject without the fear and prejudice they usually provoke.**

About the Author

Pyotr Patrushev worked for the BBC in London and as a science writer in Munich and San Francisco. He published articles in *The Sydney Morning Herald* and *The Australian* and worked for Australian radio and television.

Web: www.pyotr-patrushev.com

Blog: http://wardrugsnirvana.blogspot.com.au/

Twitter: @projectnirvana

Book: *Project Nirvana: How the War on Drugs Was Won*, Leaf Garden Press, 2014. Available on Amazon or find more information directly from the publisher at:
http://leafgardenpress.blogspot.com/2014/08/project-nirvana-how-war-on-drugs-was.html

www.ingramcontent.com/pod-product-compliance
Lightning Source LLC
Chambersburg PA
CBHW070939130626

46555CB00001B/497